MARVEL

SPIDER-

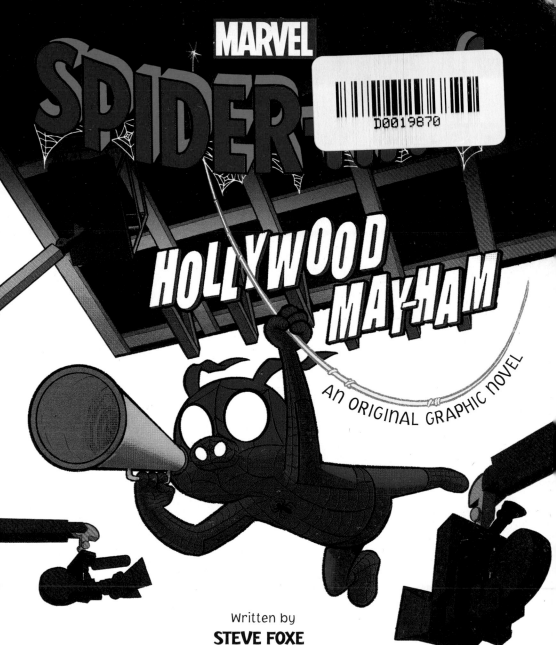

HOLLYWOOD MAY-HAM

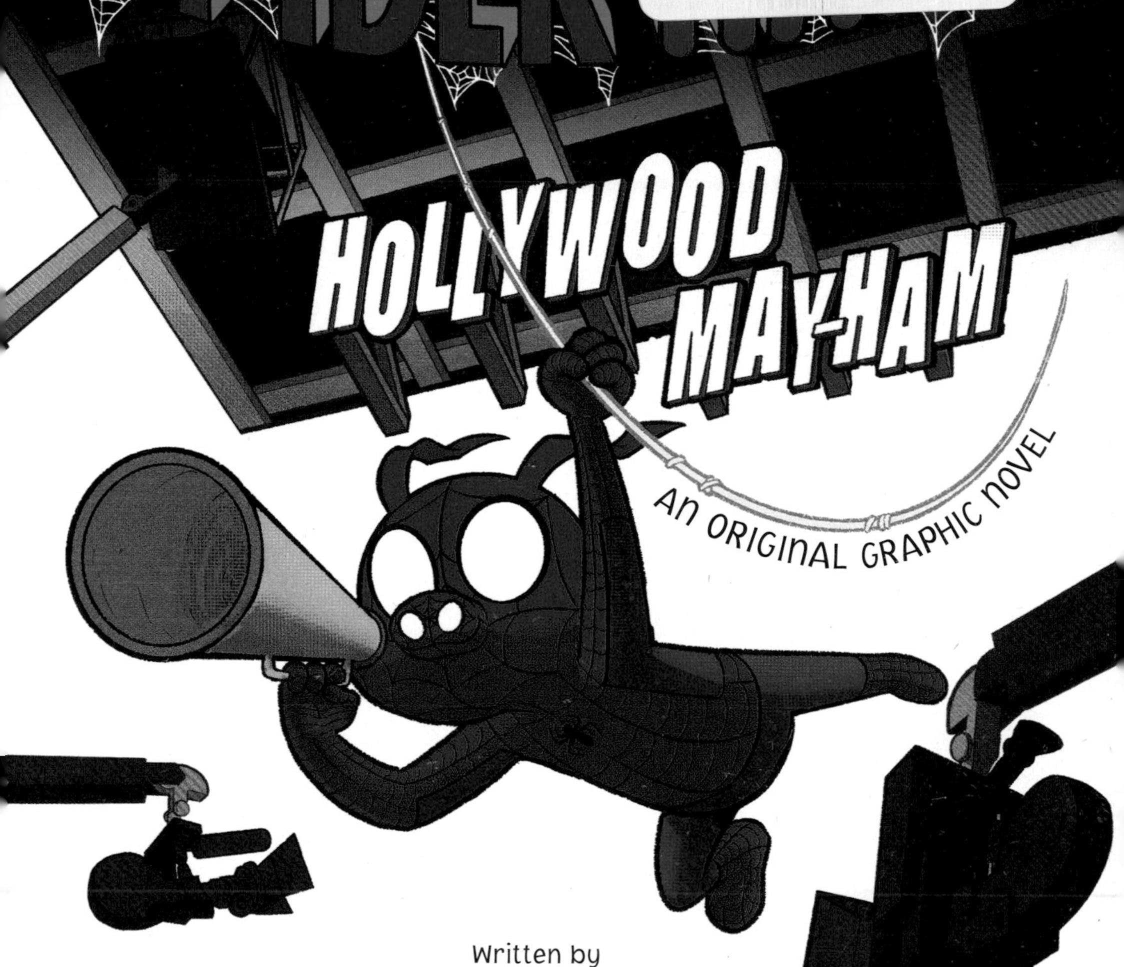

AN ORIGINAL GRAPHIC NOVEL

Written by
STEVE FOXE

Illustrated by
SHADIA AMIN

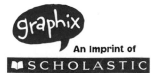

graphix
An Imprint of
SCHOLASTIC

All rights reserved. Published by Graphix, an imprint of
Scholastic Inc., *Publishers since 1920.* SCHOLASTIC, GRAPHIX,
and associated logos are trademarks and/or registered
trademarks of Scholastic Inc.

ISBN 978-1-338-80670-0 (hardcover)
ISBN 978-1-338-80669-4 (paperback)

10 9 8 7 6 5 4 3 2 1   22 23 24 25 26
Printed in China   62

First edition, October 2022

Artwork by Shadia Amin
Edited by Michael Petranek
Lettering by Rae Crawford
Book design by Jess Meltzer

Lauren Bisom, Editor, Juvenile Publishing
Caitlin O'Connell, Associate Editor
Sven Larsen, VP Licensed Publishing
C.B. Cebulski, Editor in Chief

CHAPTER ONE:

CAT BURGLAR CATASTROPHE!

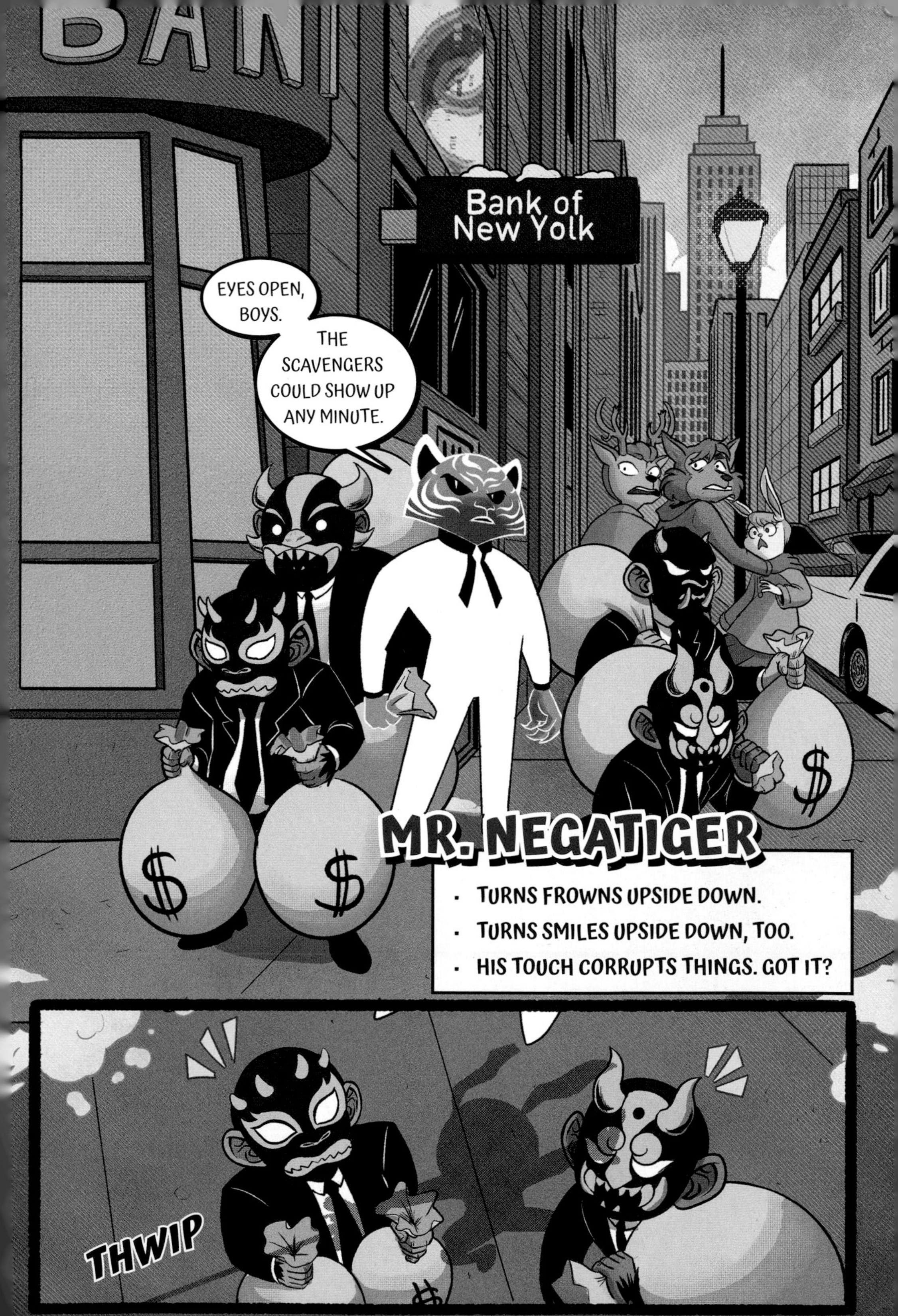
BANK
Bank of New Yolk
EYES OPEN, BOYS.
THE SCAVENGERS COULD SHOW UP ANY MINUTE.
MR. NEGATIGER
· TURNS FROWNS UPSIDE DOWN.
· TURNS SMILES UPSIDE DOWN, TOO.
· HIS TOUCH CORRUPTS THINGS. GOT IT?
THWIP

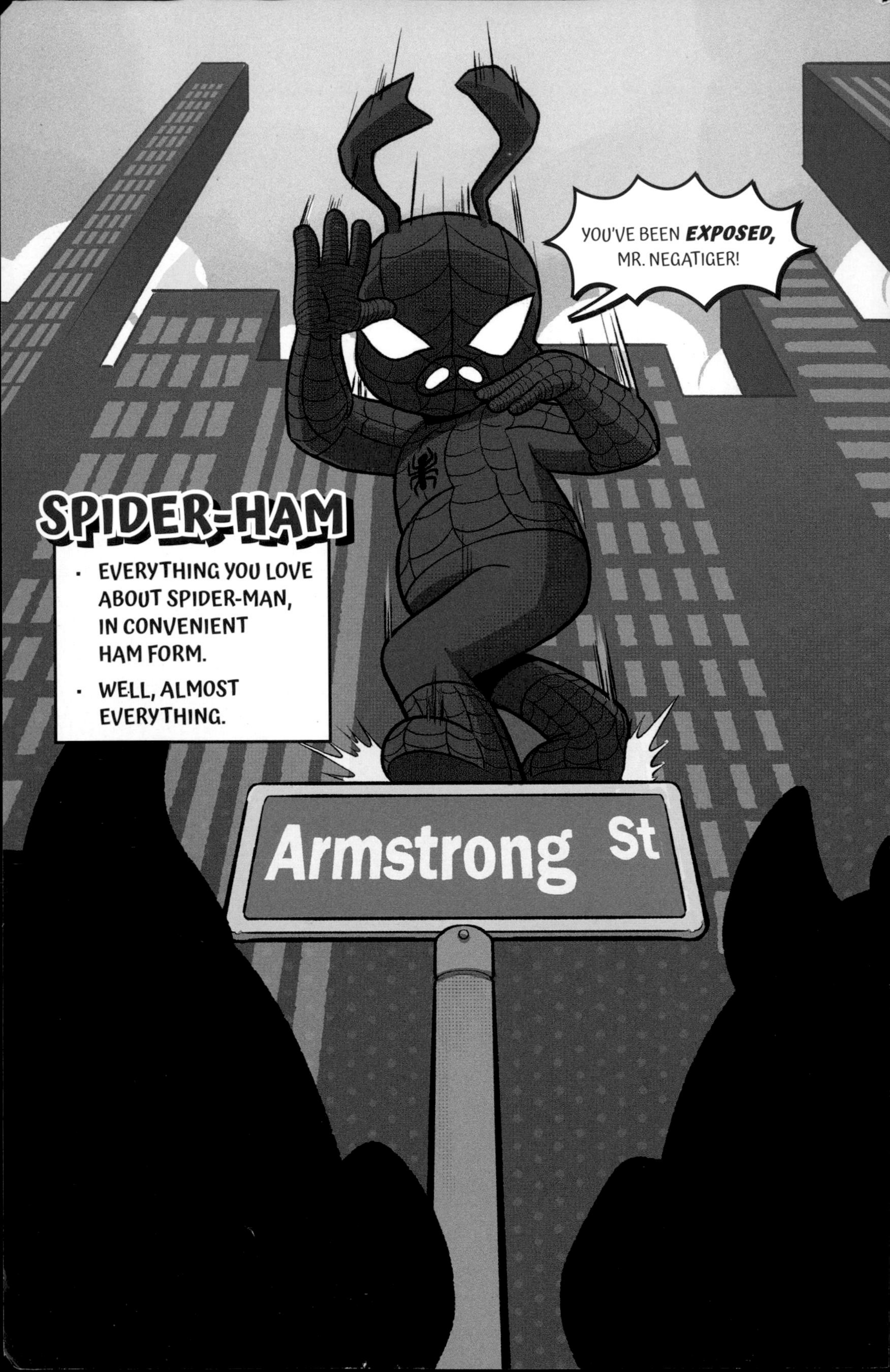
YOU'VE BEEN **EXPOSED,** MR. NEGATIGER!
SPIDER-HAM
• EVERYTHING YOU LOVE ABOUT SPIDER-MAN, IN CONVENIENT HAM FORM.
• WELL, ALMOST EVERYTHING.
Armstrong St

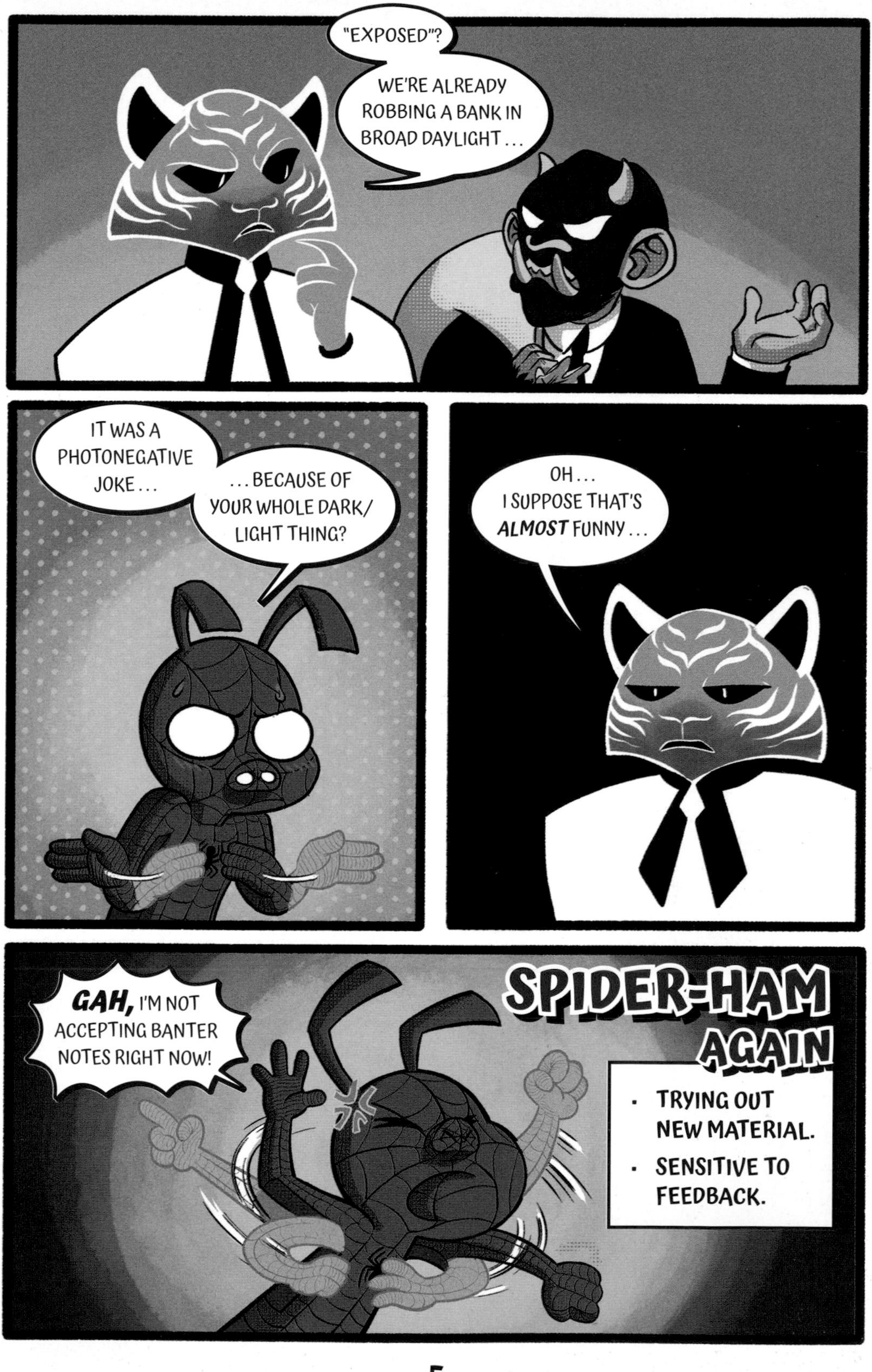

"EXPOSED"?
WE'RE ALREADY ROBBING A BANK IN BROAD DAYLIGHT . . .
IT WAS A PHOTONEGATIVE JOKE . . .
. . . BECAUSE OF YOUR WHOLE DARK/ LIGHT THING?
OH . . . I SUPPOSE THAT'S **ALMOST** FUNNY . . .
GAH, I'M NOT ACCEPTING BANTER NOTES RIGHT NOW!
SPIDER-HAM AGAIN
• TRYING OUT NEW MATERIAL.
• SENSITIVE TO FEEDBACK.

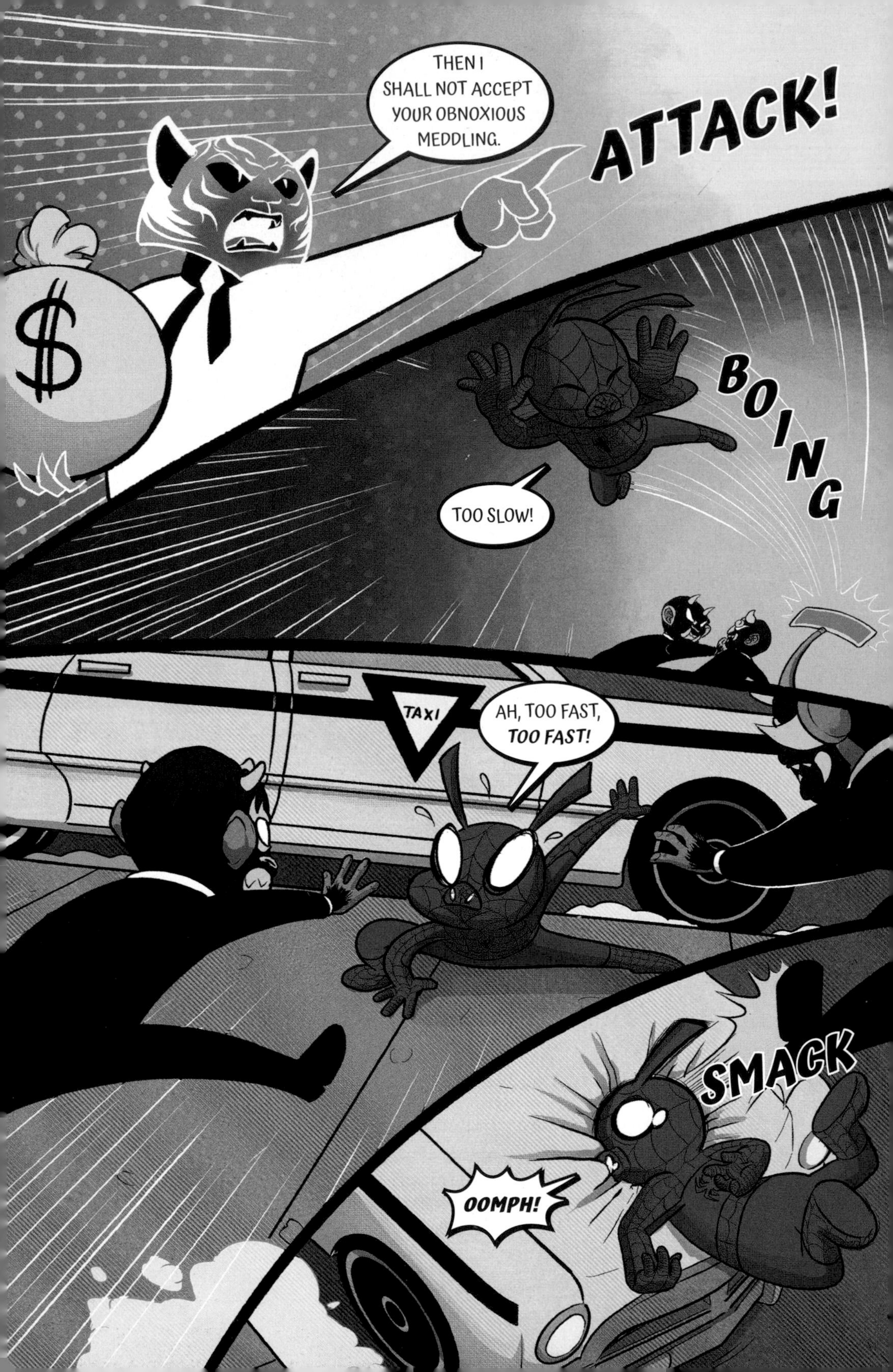
THEN I SHALL NOT ACCEPT YOUR OBNOXIOUS MEDDLING.
ATTACK!
BOING
TOO SLOW!
TAXI
AH, TOO FAST, *TOO FAST!*
SMACK
OOMPH!

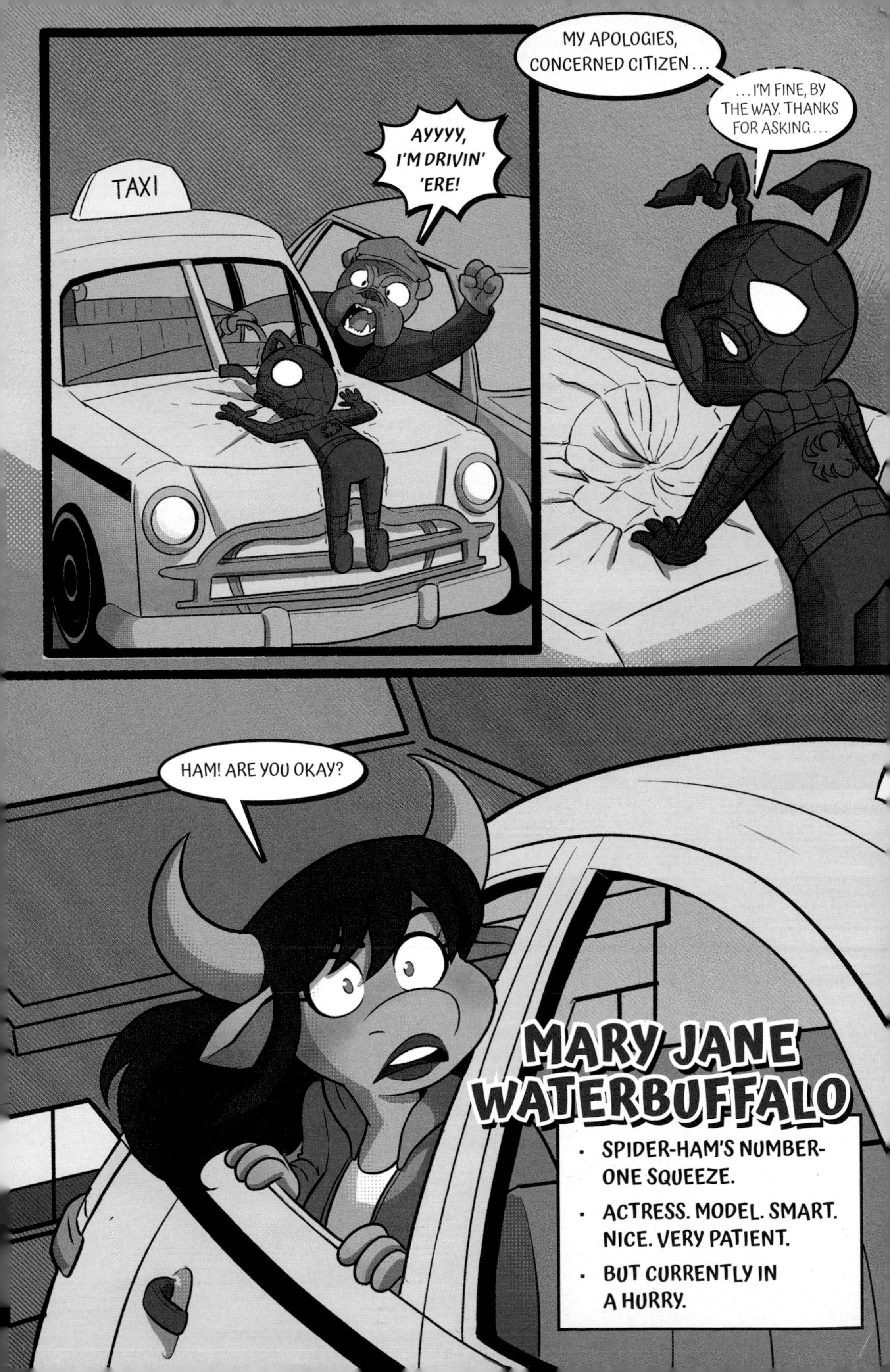
AYYYY, I'M DRIVIN' 'ERE!
TAXI
MY APOLOGIES, CONCERNED CITIZEN . . .
. . . I'M FINE, BY THE WAY. THANKS FOR ASKING . . .
HAM! ARE YOU OKAY?
MARY JANE WATERBUFFALO
· SPIDER-HAM'S NUMBER-ONE SQUEEZE.
· ACTRESS. MODEL. SMART. NICE. VERY PATIENT.
· BUT CURRENTLY IN A HURRY.

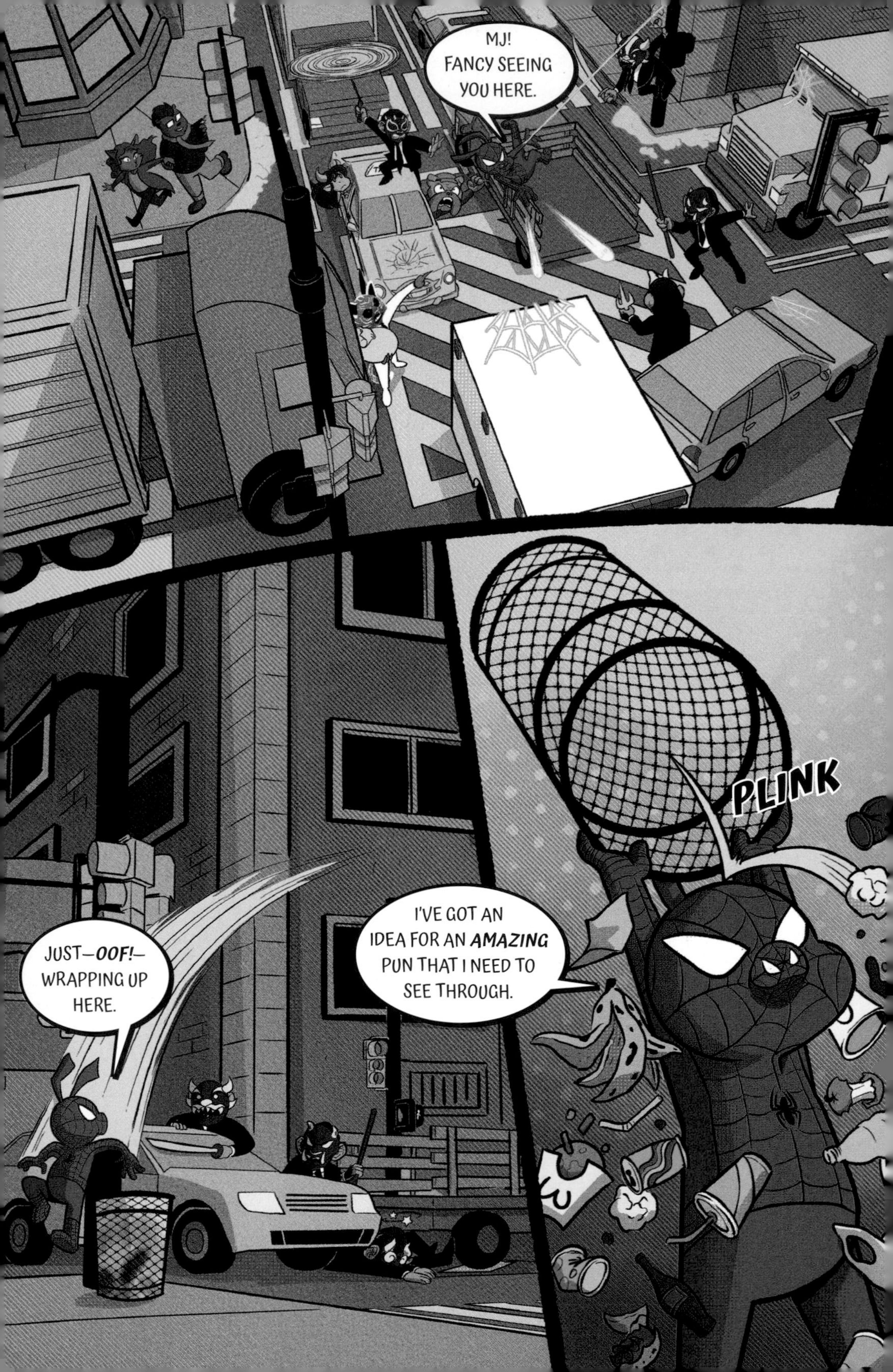
MJ! FANCY SEEING YOU HERE.
JUST—*OOF!*—WRAPPING UP HERE.
I'VE GOT AN IDEA FOR AN ***AMAZING*** PUN THAT I NEED TO SEE THROUGH.
PLINK

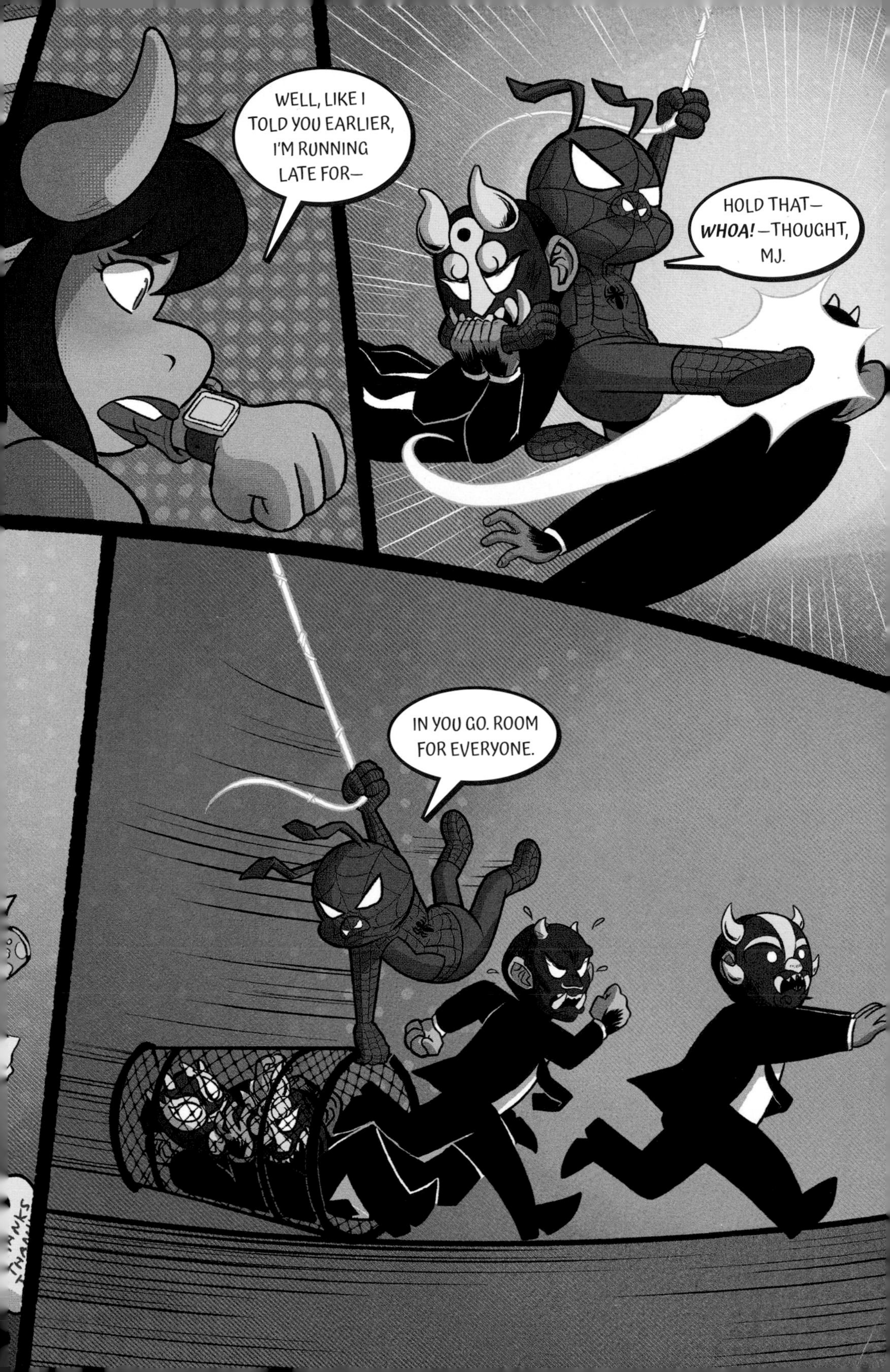
WELL, LIKE I TOLD YOU EARLIER, I'M RUNNING LATE FOR—
HOLD THAT— ***WHOA!*** —THOUGHT, MJ.
IN YOU GO. ROOM FOR EVERYONE.

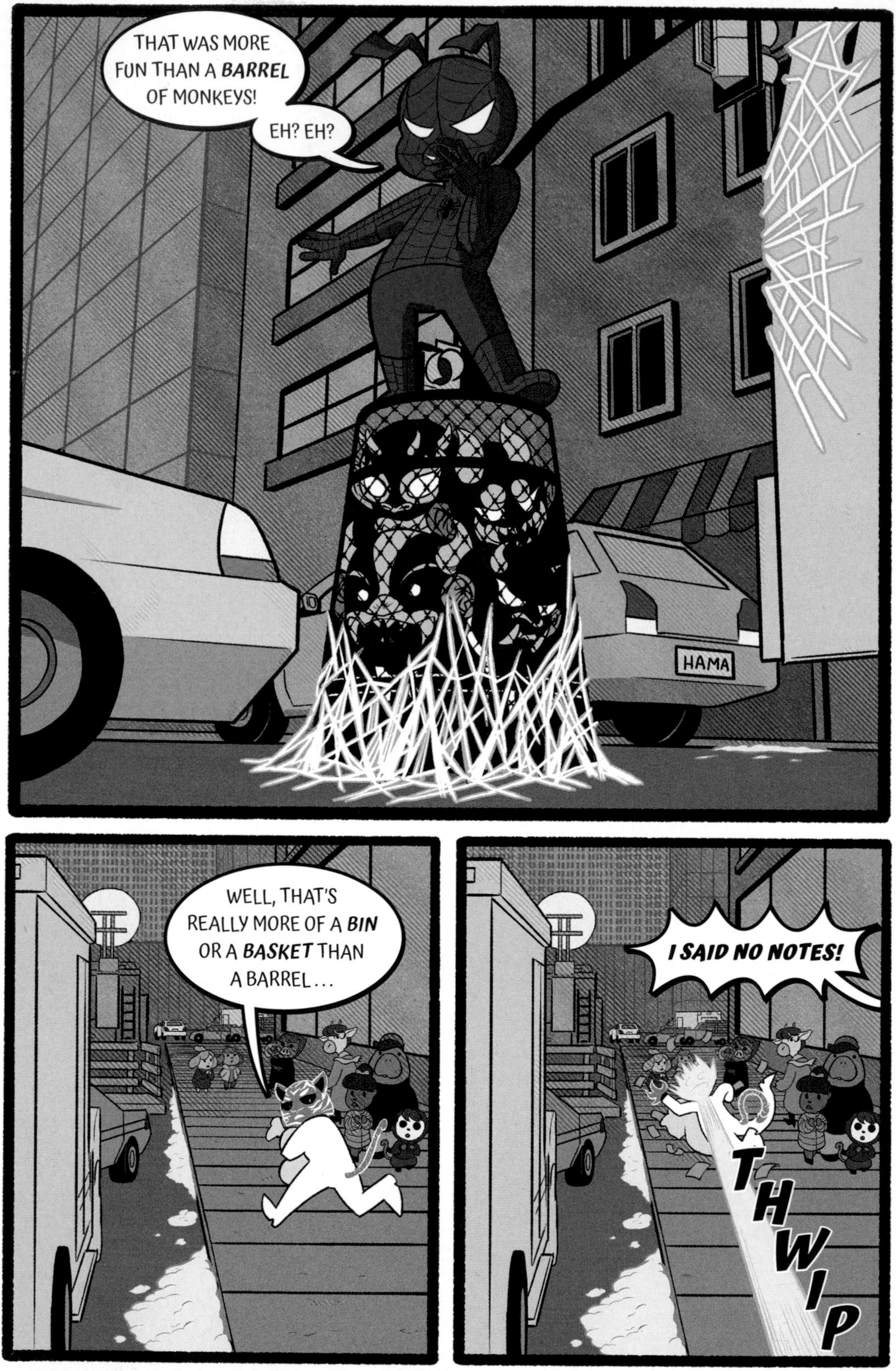
THAT WAS MORE FUN THAN A BARREL OF MONKEYS!
EH? EH?
HAMA
WELL, THAT'S REALLY MORE OF A BIN OR A BASKET THAN A BARREL...
I SAID NO NOTES!
THWIP

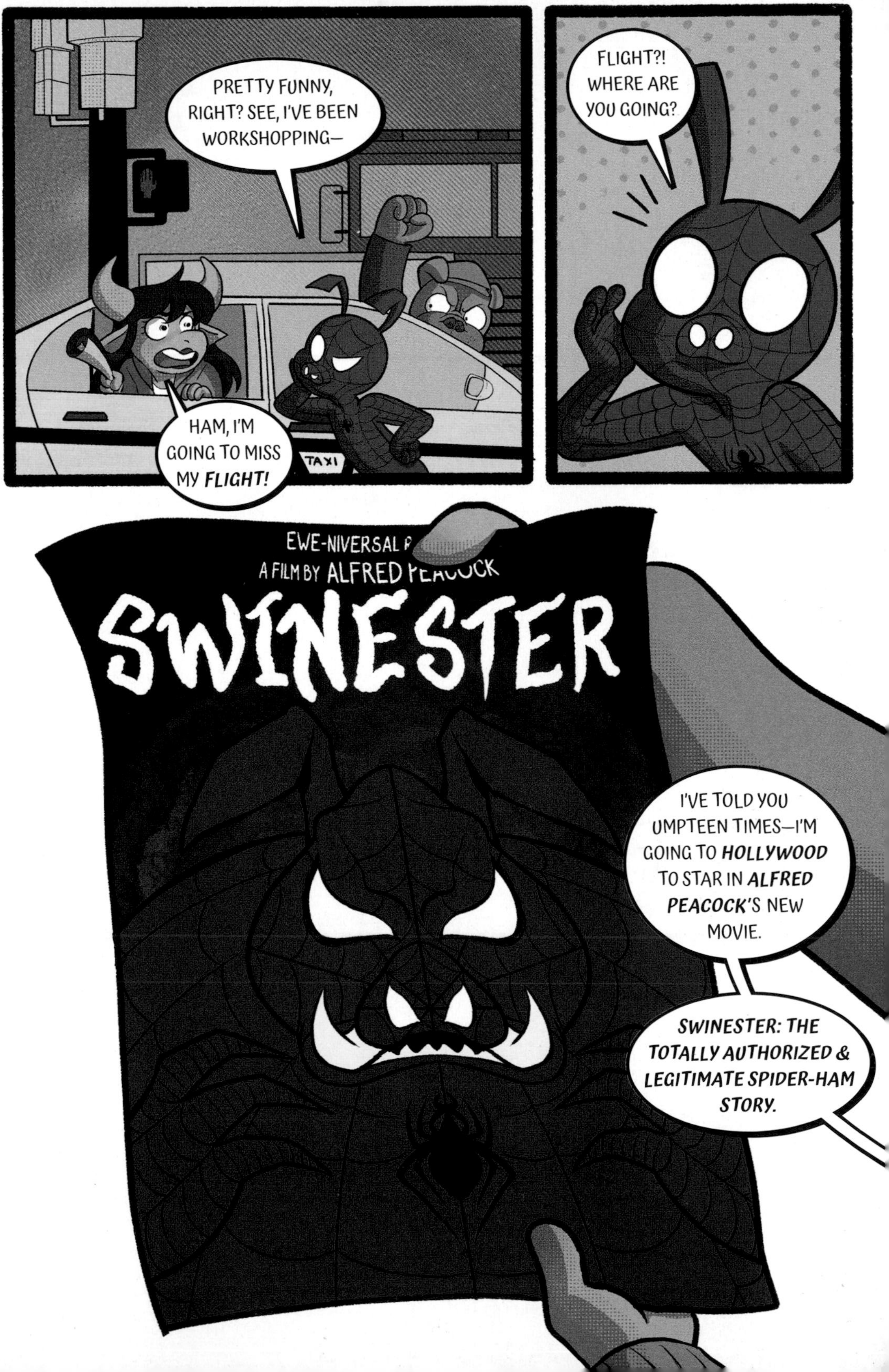
PRETTY FUNNY, RIGHT? SEE, I'VE BEEN WORKSHOPPING—
HAM, I'M GOING TO MISS MY FLIGHT!
TAXI
FLIGHT?! WHERE ARE YOU GOING?
EWE-NIVERSAL P
A FILM BY ALFRED PEACOCK
SWINESTER
I'VE TOLD YOU UMPTEEN TIMES—I'M GOING TO HOLLYWOOD TO STAR IN ALFRED PEACOCK'S NEW MOVIE.
SWINESTER: THE TOTALLY AUTHORIZED & LEGITIMATE SPIDER-HAM STORY.

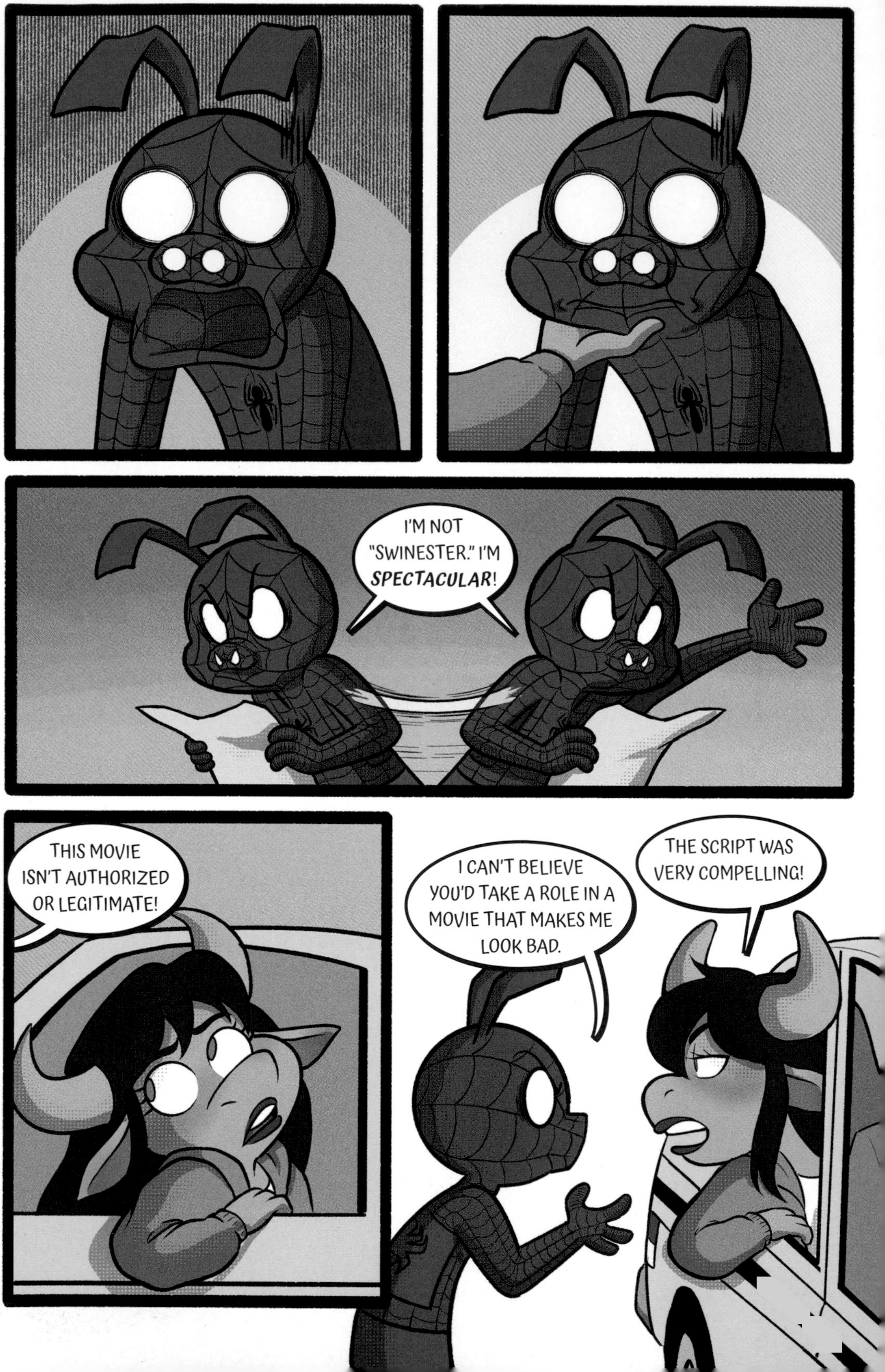
I'M NOT "SWINESTER." I'M *SPECTACULAR*!
THIS MOVIE ISN'T AUTHORIZED OR LEGITIMATE!
I CAN'T BELIEVE YOU'D TAKE A ROLE IN A MOVIE THAT MAKES ME LOOK BAD.
THE SCRIPT WAS VERY COMPELLING!

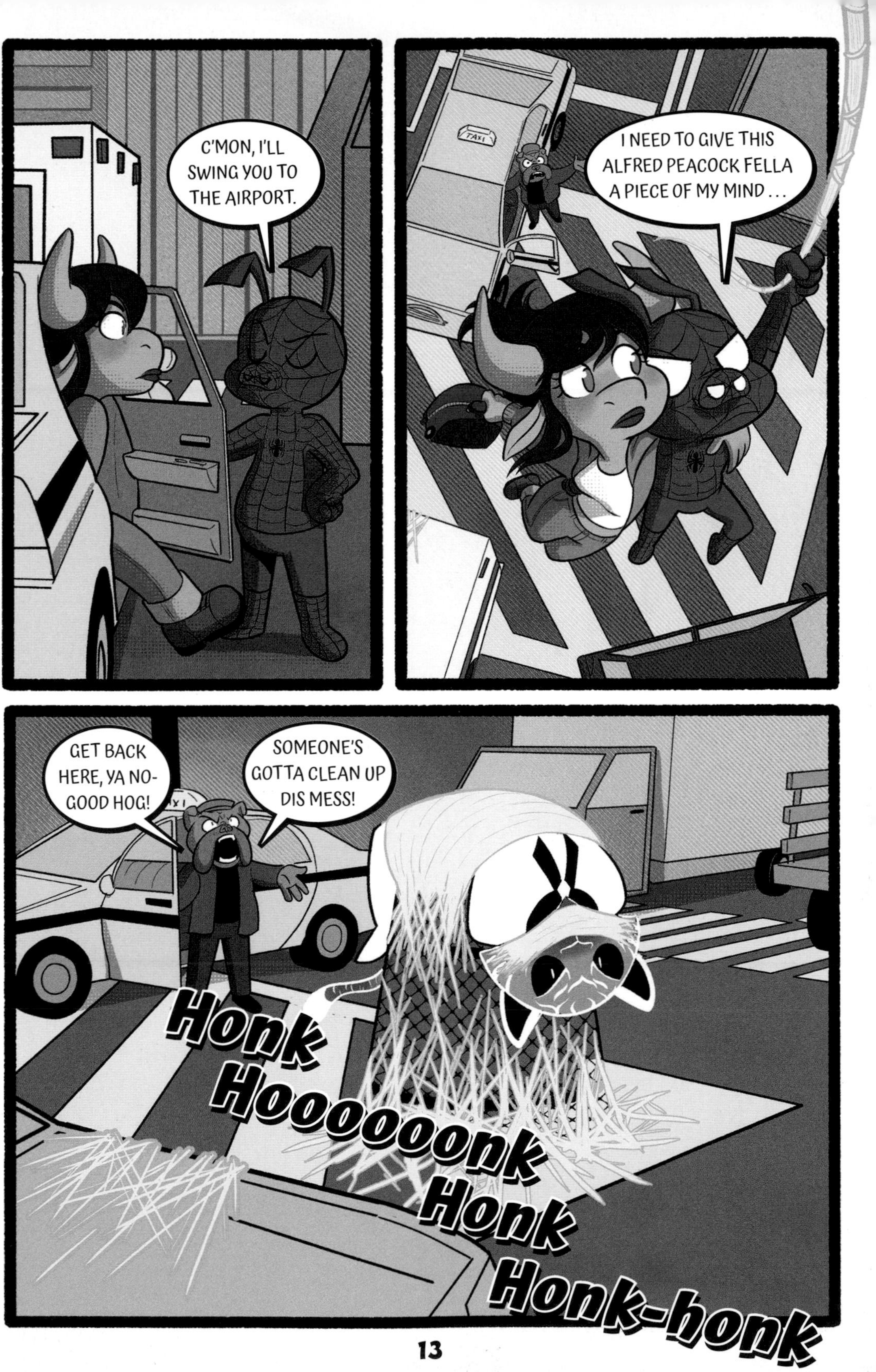
C'MON, I'LL SWING YOU TO THE AIRPORT.
TAXI
I NEED TO GIVE THIS ALFRED PEACOCK FELLA A PIECE OF MY MIND . . .
GET BACK HERE, YA NO-GOOD HOG!
SOMEONE'S GOTTA CLEAN UP DIS MESS!
Honk
Hoooooooonk
Honk
Honk-honk

CHAPTER TWO:
PIGCOGNITO!

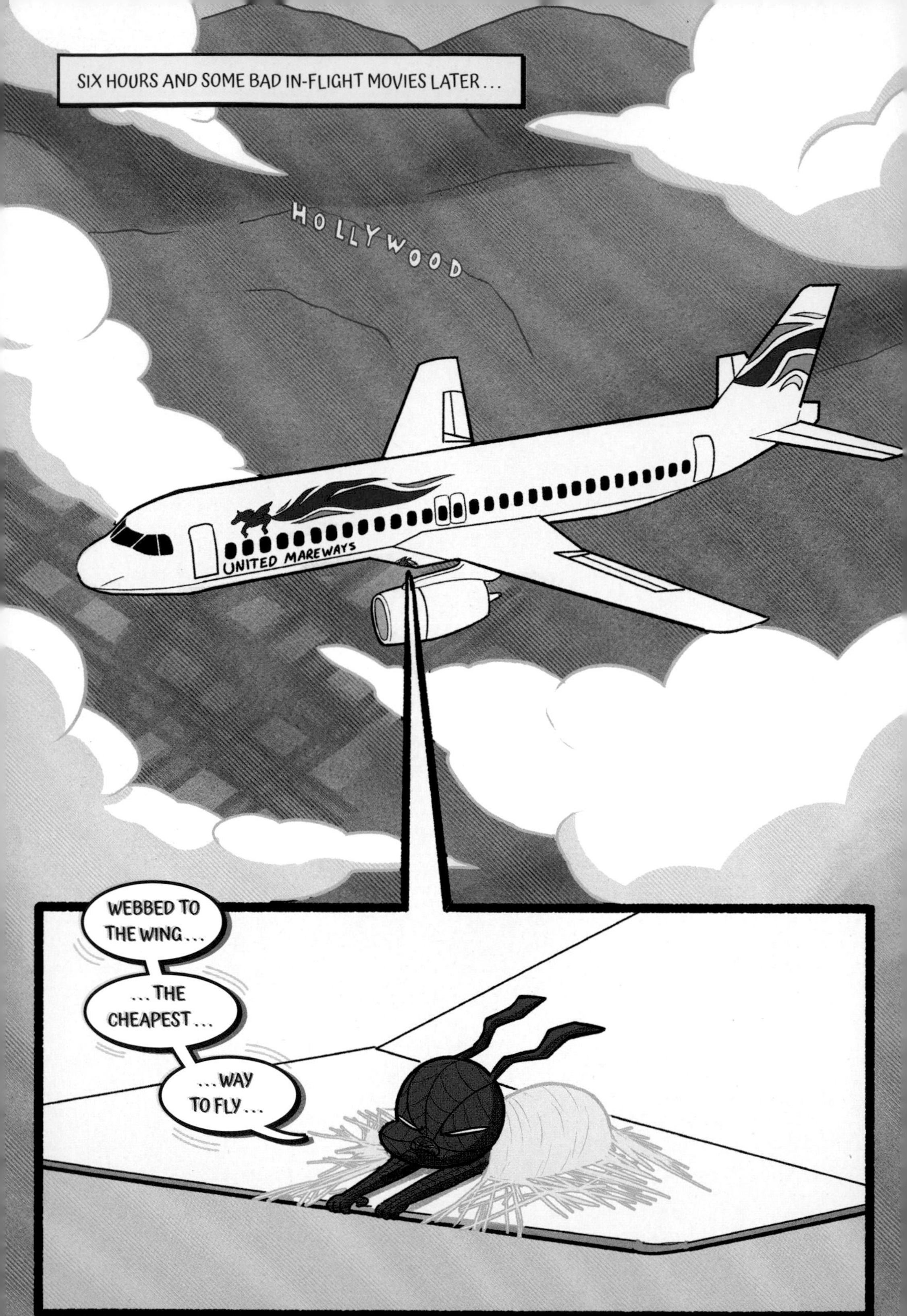

SIX HOURS AND SOME BAD IN-FLIGHT MOVIES LATER...
HOLLYWOOD
UNITED MAREWAYS
WEBBED TO THE WING...
...THE CHEAPEST...
...WAY TO FLY...

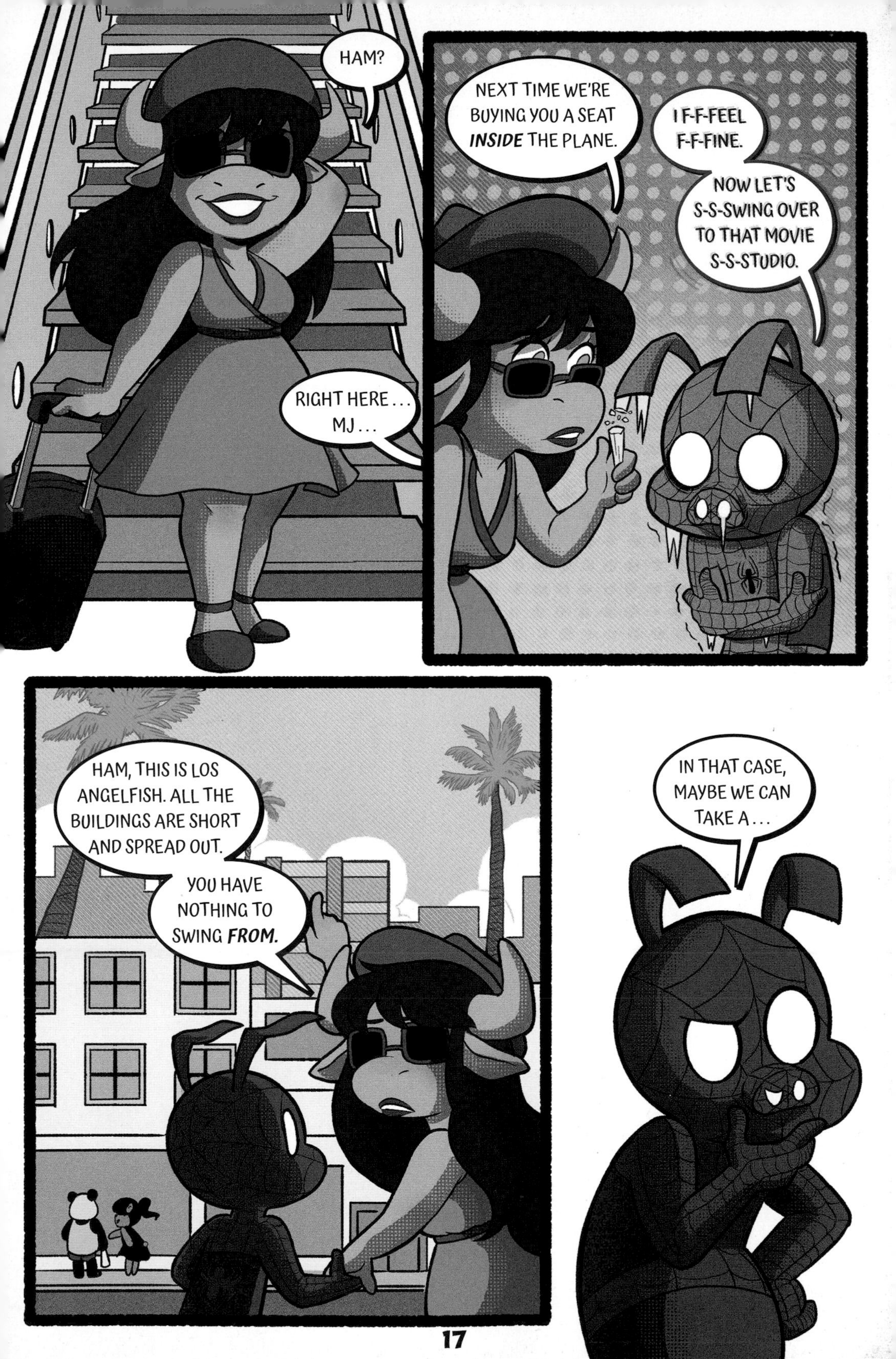
HAM?
RIGHT HERE . . . MJ . . .
NEXT TIME WE'RE BUYING YOU A SEAT **INSIDE** THE PLANE.
I F-F-FEEL F-F-FINE.
NOW LET'S S-S-SWING OVER TO THAT MOVIE S-S-STUDIO.
HAM, THIS IS LOS ANGELFISH. ALL THE BUILDINGS ARE SHORT AND SPREAD OUT.
YOU HAVE NOTHING TO SWING **FROM.**
IN THAT CASE, MAYBE WE CAN TAKE A . . .

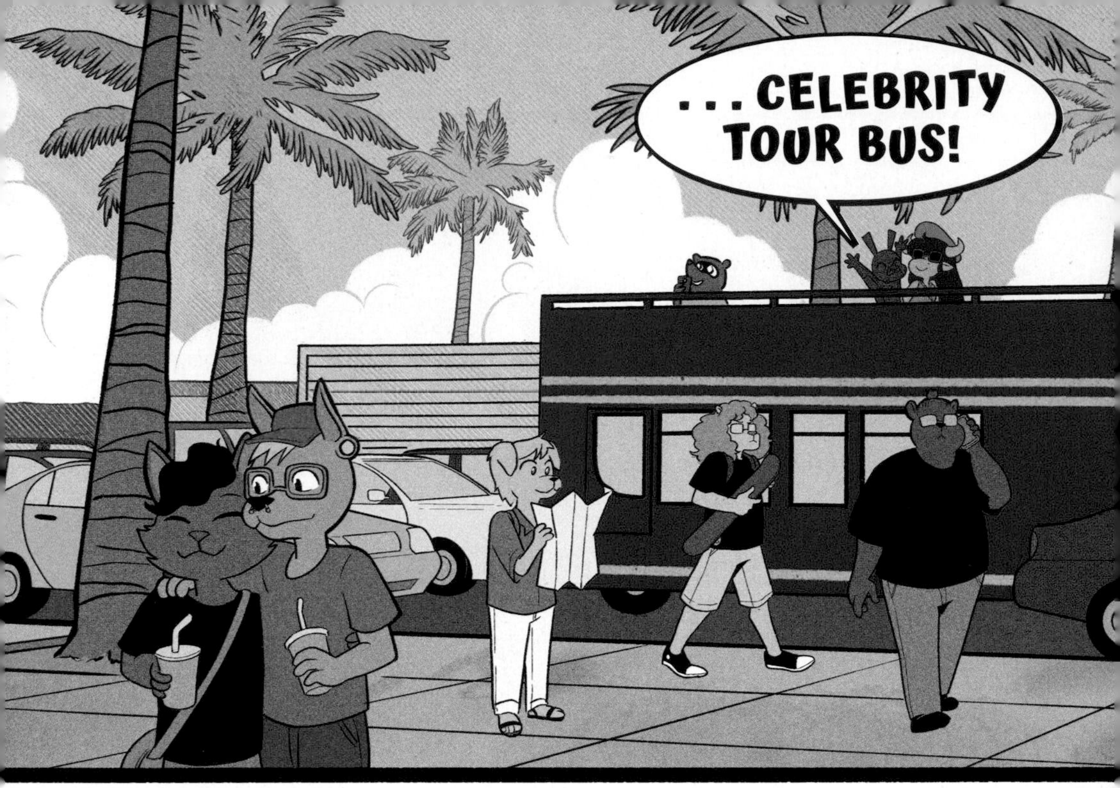
...CELEBRITY TOUR BUS!

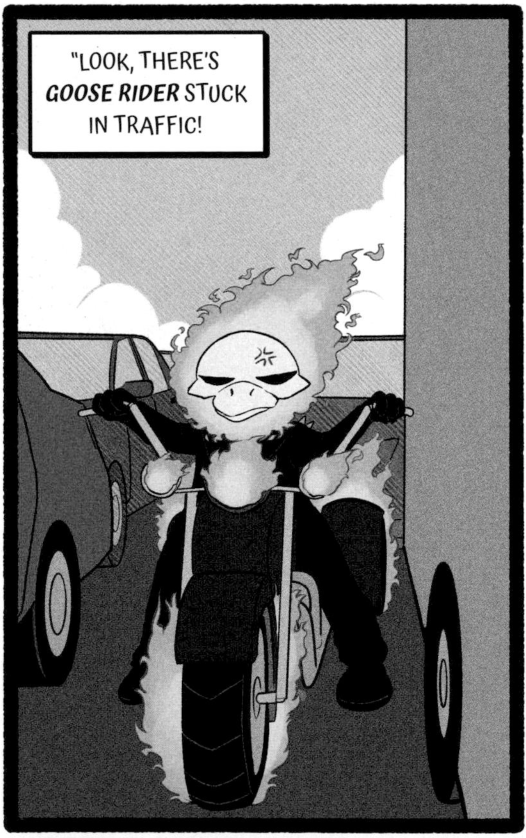
"LOOK, THERE'S GOOSE RIDER STUCK IN TRAFFIC!

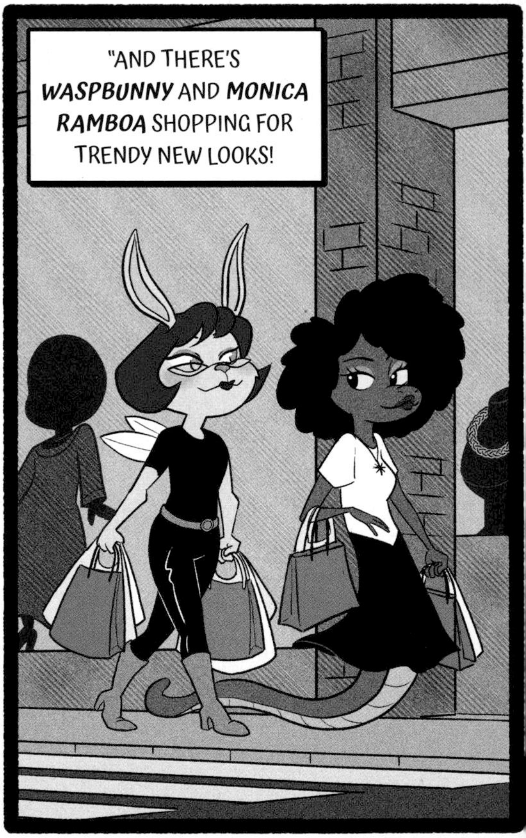
"AND THERE'S WASPBUNNY AND MONICA RAMBOA SHOPPING FOR TRENDY NEW LOOKS!

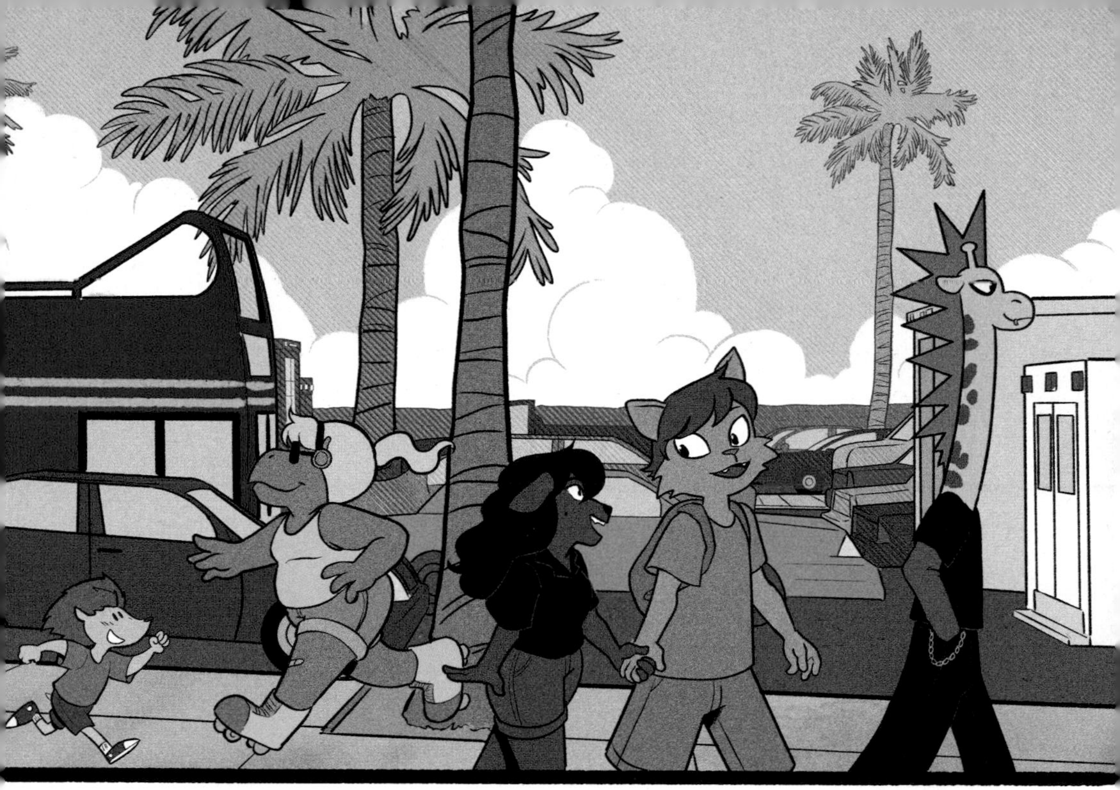

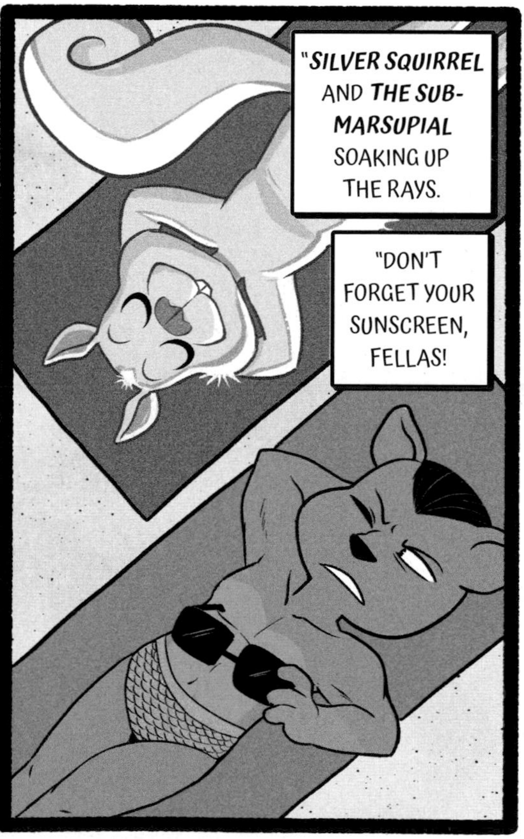
"SILVER SQUIRREL AND THE SUB-MARSUPIAL SOAKING UP THE RAYS.
"DON'T FORGET YOUR SUNSCREEN, FELLAS!

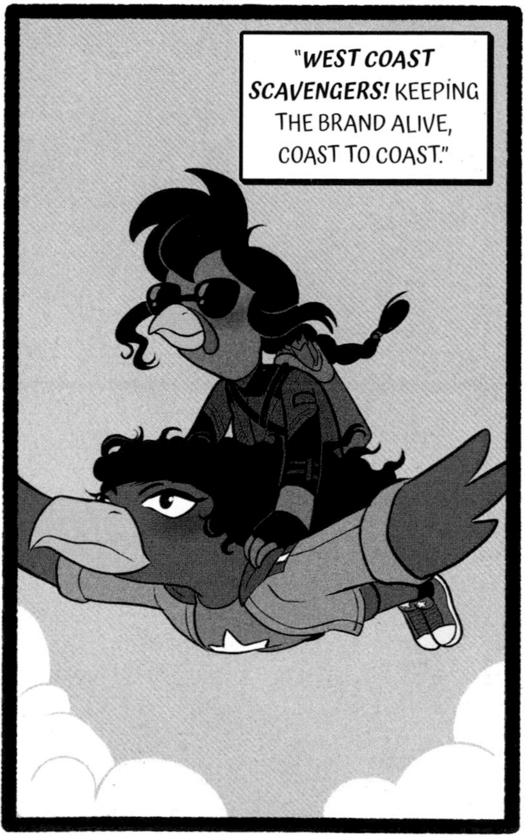
"WEST COAST SCAVENGERS! KEEPING THE BRAND ALIVE, COAST TO COAST."

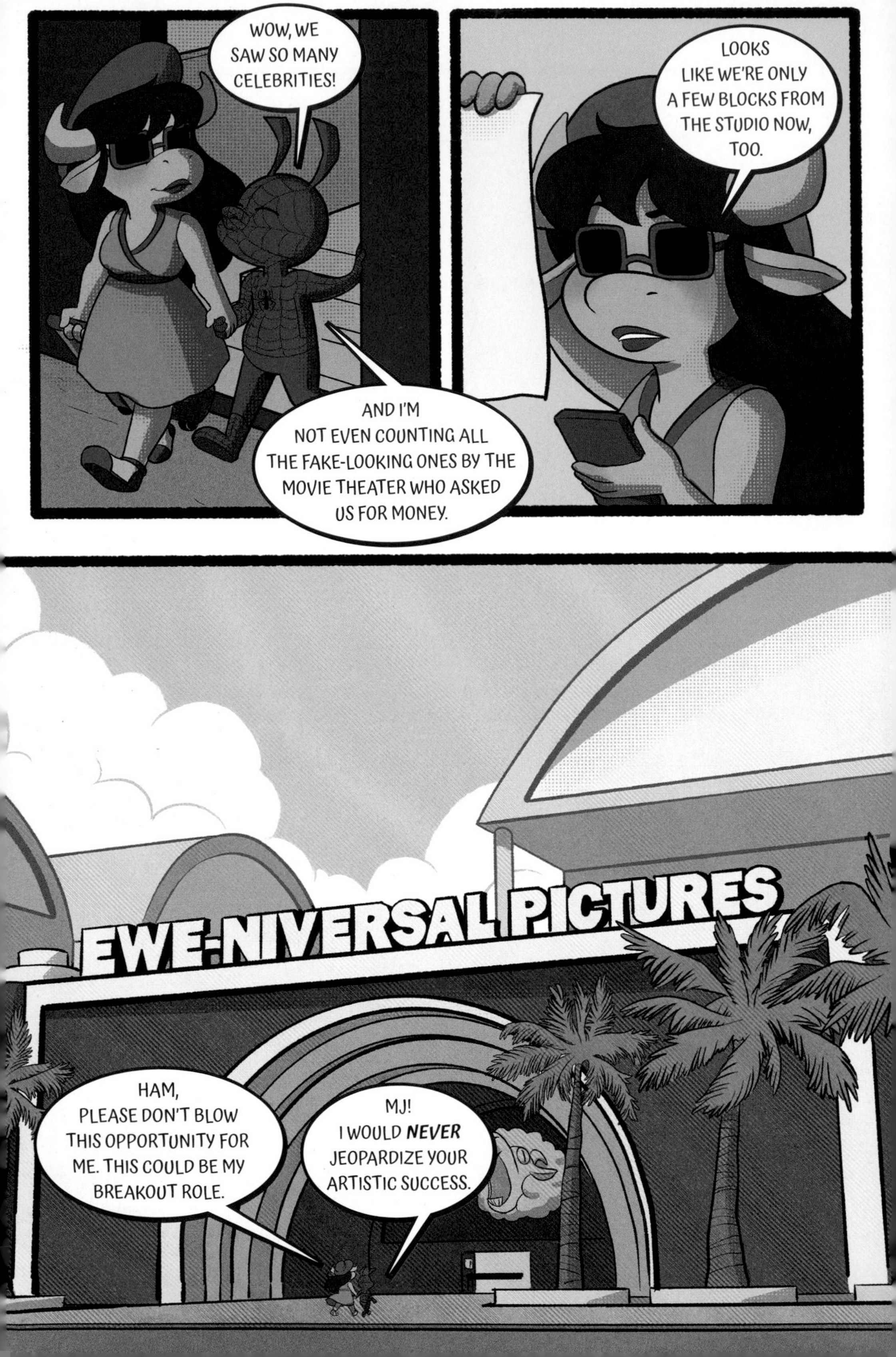
WOW, WE SAW SO MANY CELEBRITIES!
AND I'M NOT EVEN COUNTING ALL THE FAKE-LOOKING ONES BY THE MOVIE THEATER WHO ASKED US FOR MONEY.
LOOKS LIKE WE'RE ONLY A FEW BLOCKS FROM THE STUDIO NOW, TOO.
EWE-NIVERSAL PICTURES
HAM, PLEASE DON'T BLOW THIS OPPORTUNITY FOR ME. THIS COULD BE MY BREAKOUT ROLE.
MJ! I WOULD ***NEVER*** JEOPARDIZE YOUR ARTISTIC SUCCESS.

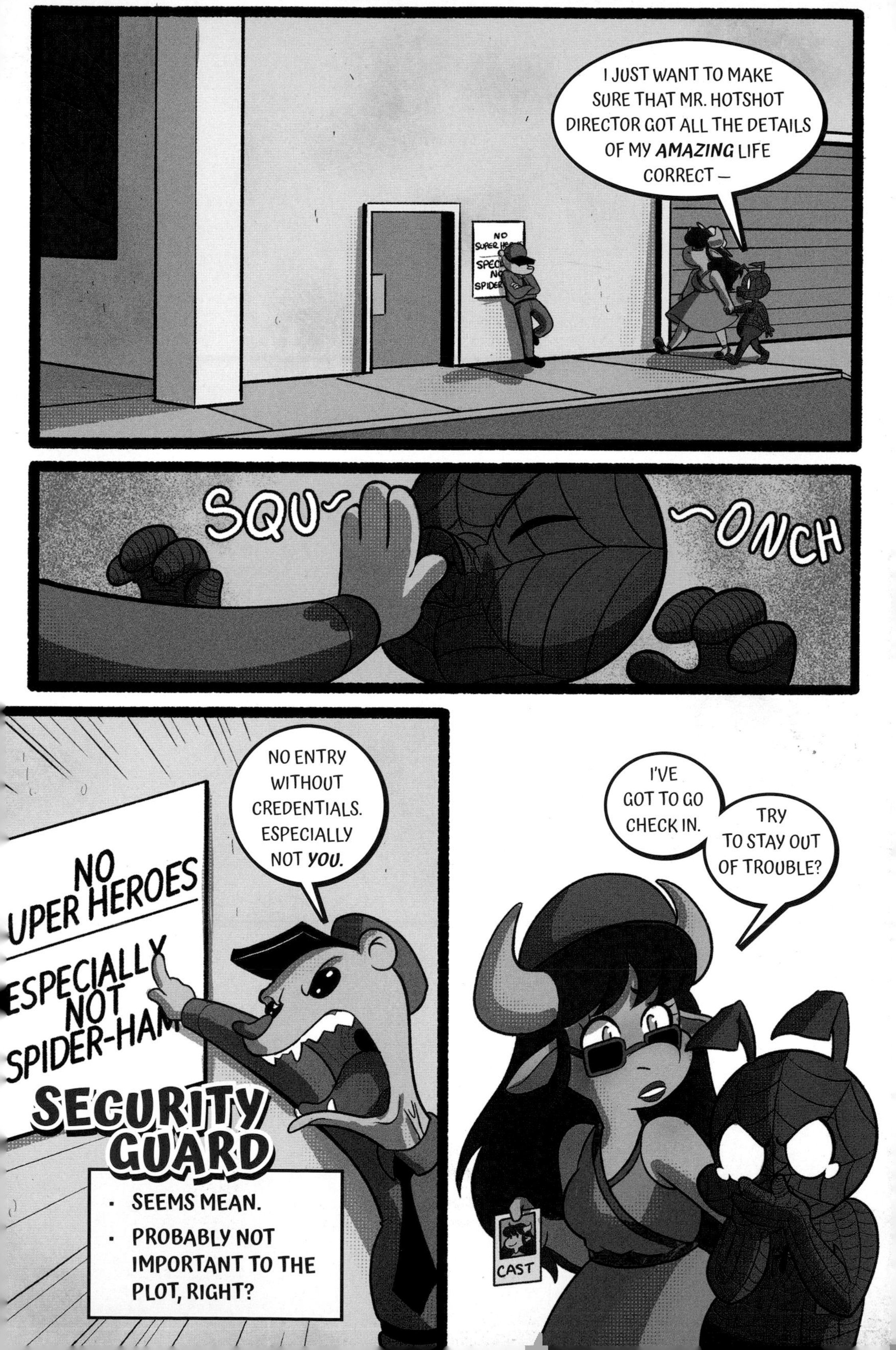
I JUST WANT TO MAKE SURE THAT MR. HOTSHOT DIRECTOR GOT ALL THE DETAILS OF MY AMAZING LIFE CORRECT —
NO SUPER HEROES SPECI NO SPIDER
SQU~
~ONCH
NO ENTRY WITHOUT CREDENTIALS. ESPECIALLY NOT YOU.
NO UPER HEROES
ESPECIALLY NOT SPIDER-HAM
SECURITY GUARD
• SEEMS MEAN.
• PROBABLY NOT IMPORTANT TO THE PLOT, RIGHT?
I'VE GOT TO GO CHECK IN.
TRY TO STAY OUT OF TROUBLE?
CAST

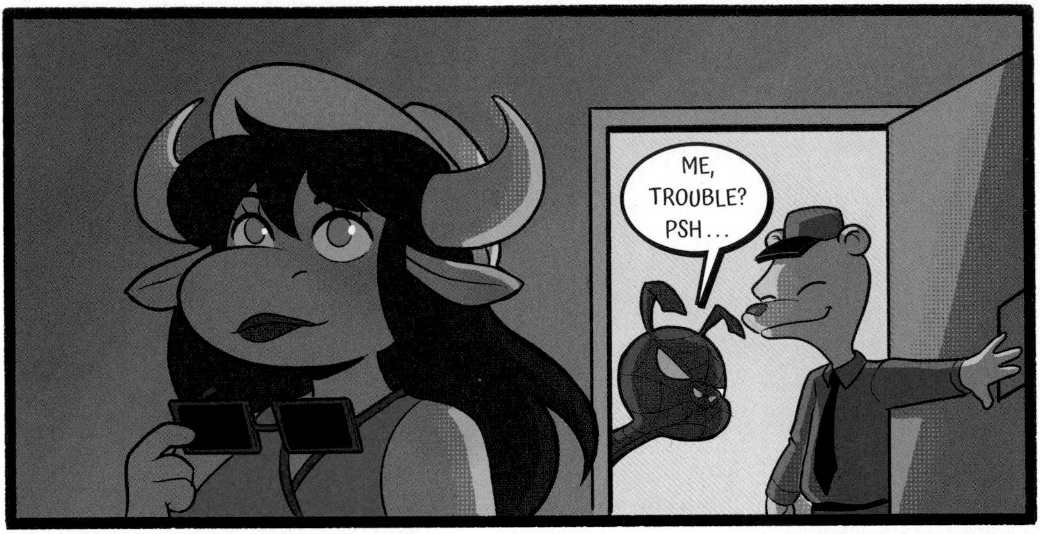
ME, TROUBLE? PSH...

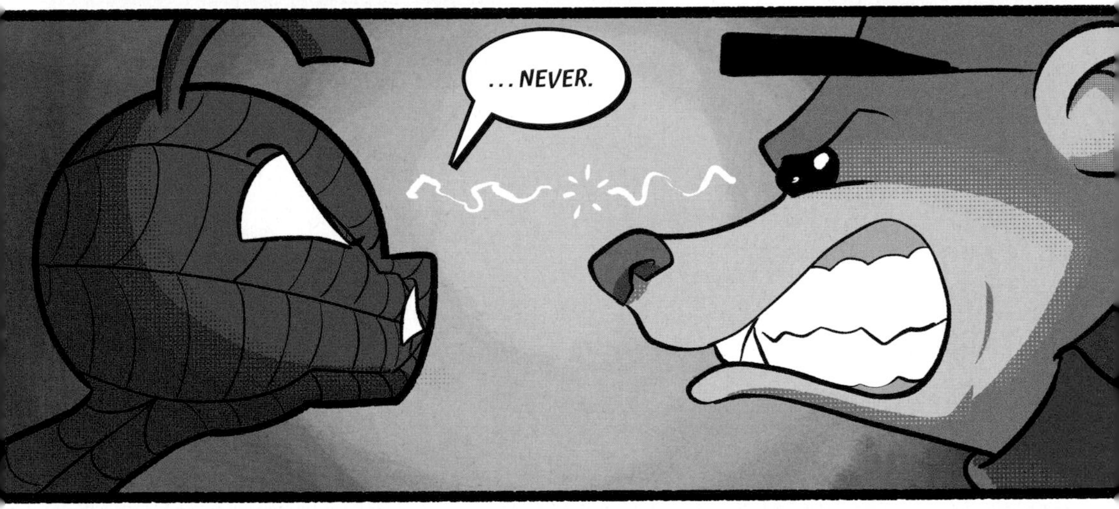
...NEVER.

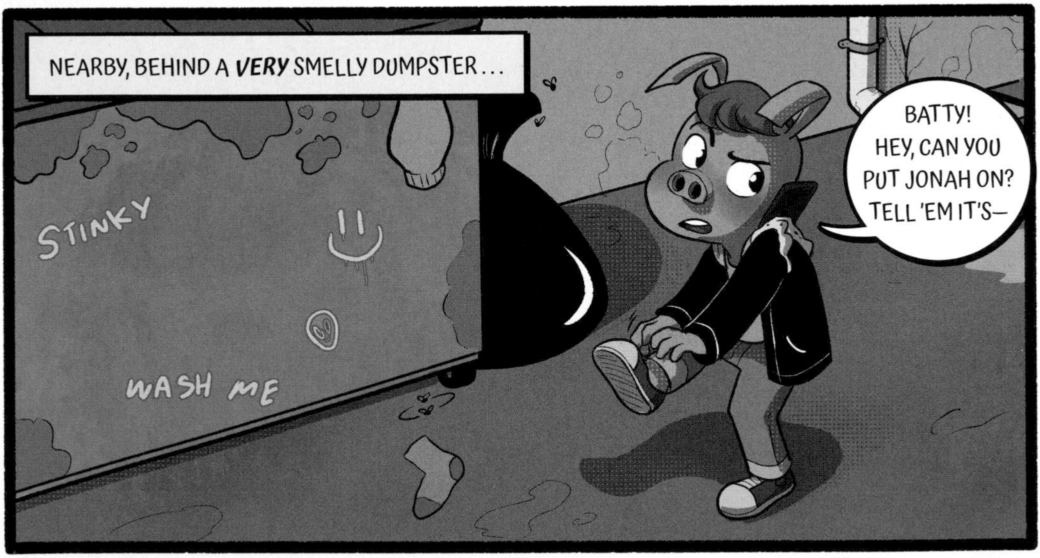
NEARBY, BEHIND A VERY SMELLY DUMPSTER...
STINKY
WASH ME
BATTY! HEY, CAN YOU PUT JONAH ON? TELL 'EM IT'S—

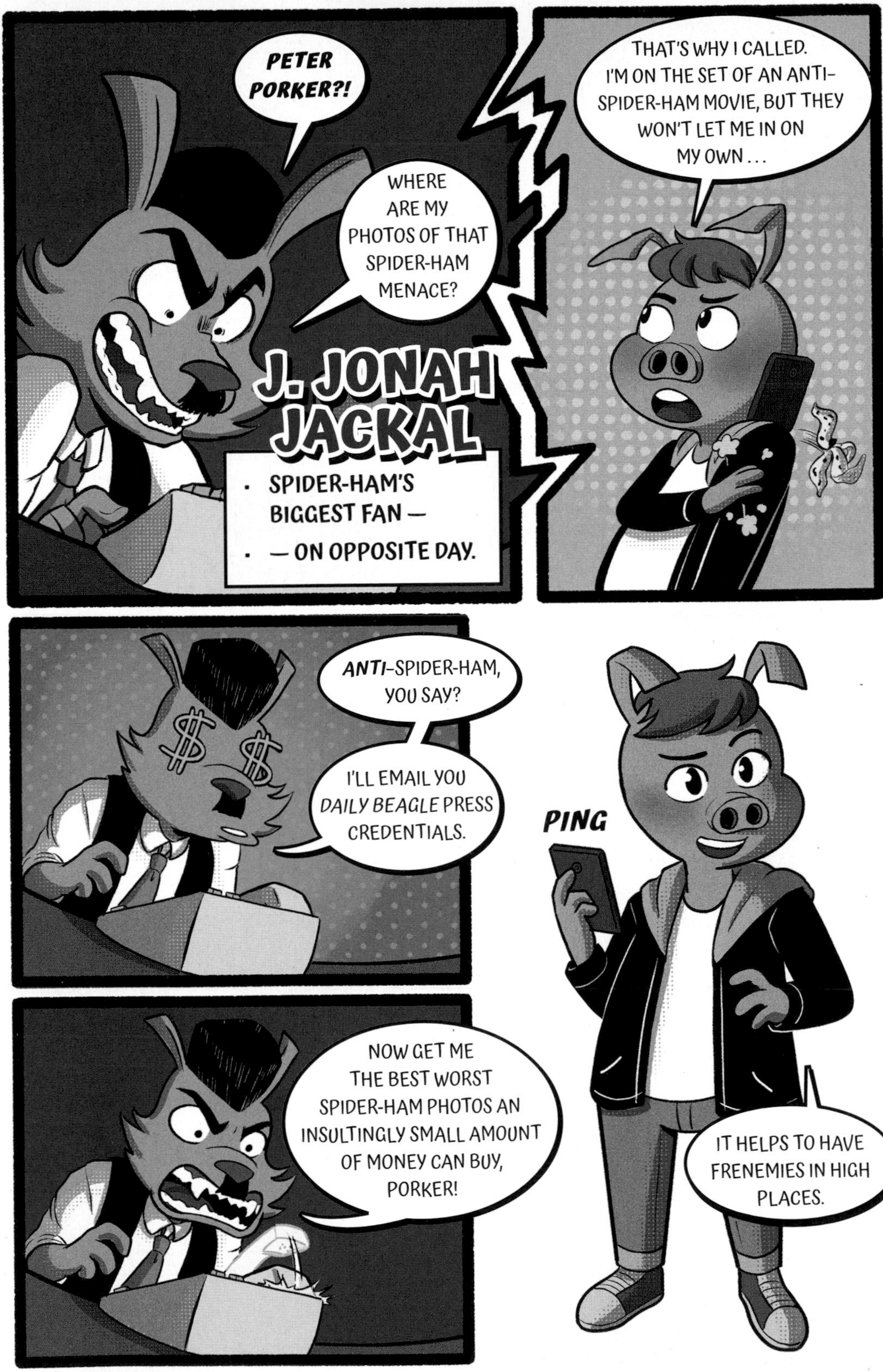
PETER PORKER?!
WHERE ARE MY PHOTOS OF THAT SPIDER-HAM MENACE?
J. JONAH JACKAL
• SPIDER-HAM'S BIGGEST FAN —
• — ON OPPOSITE DAY.
THAT'S WHY I CALLED. I'M ON THE SET OF AN ANTI-SPIDER-HAM MOVIE, BUT THEY WON'T LET ME IN ON MY OWN . . .
ANTI-SPIDER-HAM, YOU SAY?
I'LL EMAIL YOU *DAILY BEAGLE* PRESS CREDENTIALS.
PING
NOW GET ME THE BEST WORST SPIDER-HAM PHOTOS AN INSULTINGLY SMALL AMOUNT OF MONEY CAN BUY, PORKER!
IT HELPS TO HAVE FRENEMIES IN HIGH PLACES.

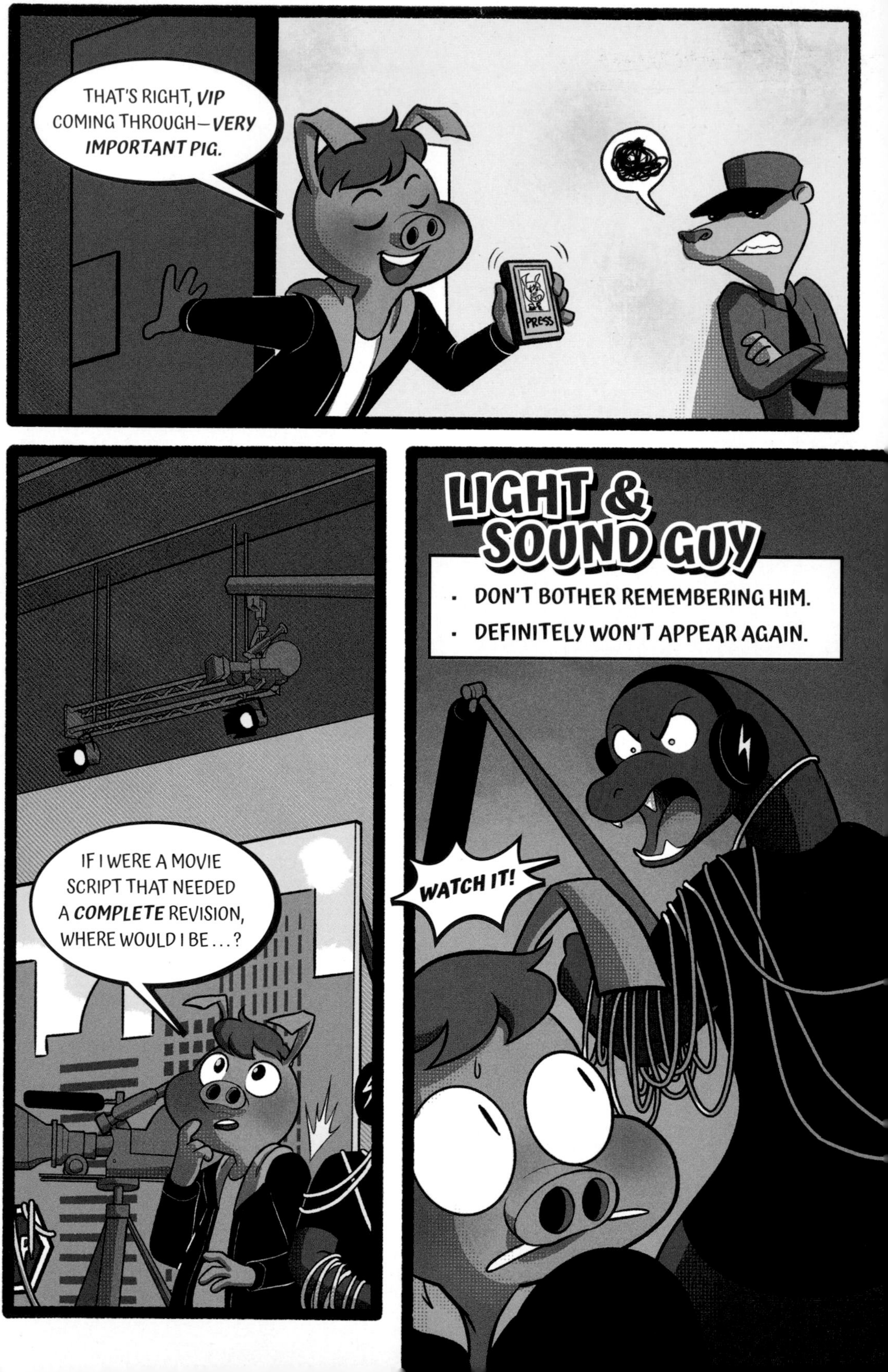
THAT'S RIGHT, VIP COMING THROUGH—VERY IMPORTANT PIG.
PRESS
IF I WERE A MOVIE SCRIPT THAT NEEDED A COMPLETE REVISION, WHERE WOULD I BE . . . ?
LIGHT & SOUND GUY
• DON'T BOTHER REMEMBERING HIM.
• DEFINITELY WON'T APPEAR AGAIN.
WATCH IT!

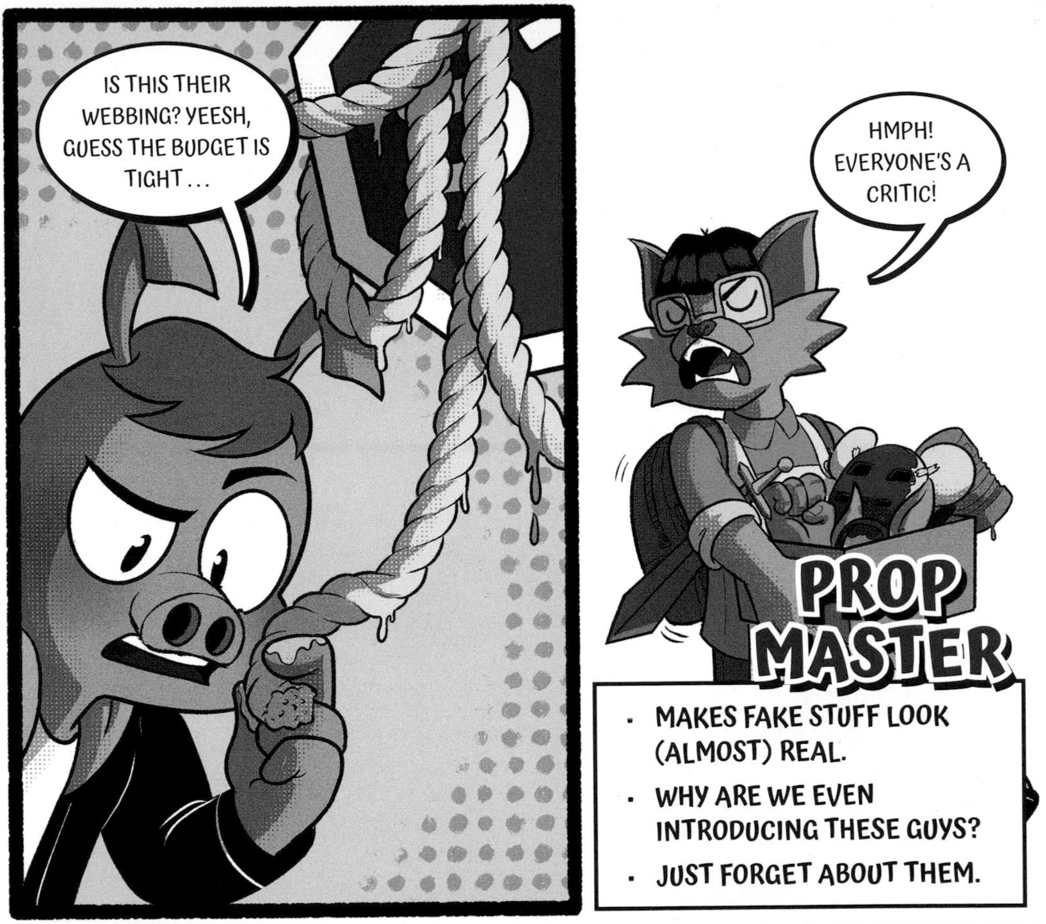
IS THIS THEIR WEBBING? YEESH, GUESS THE BUDGET IS TIGHT . . .
HMPH! EVERYONE'S A CRITIC!
PROP MASTER
• MAKES FAKE STUFF LOOK (ALMOST) REAL.
• WHY ARE WE EVEN INTRODUCING THESE GUYS?
• JUST FORGET ABOUT THEM.

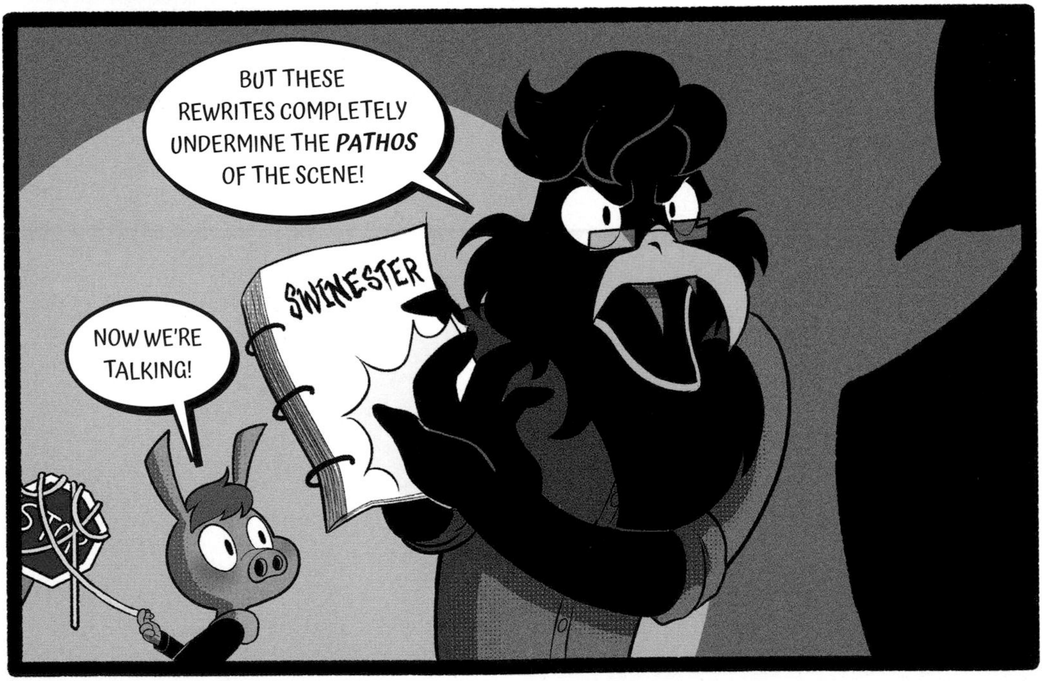
BUT THESE REWRITES COMPLETELY UNDERMINE THE *PATHOS* OF THE SCENE!
SWINESTER
NOW WE'RE TALKING!

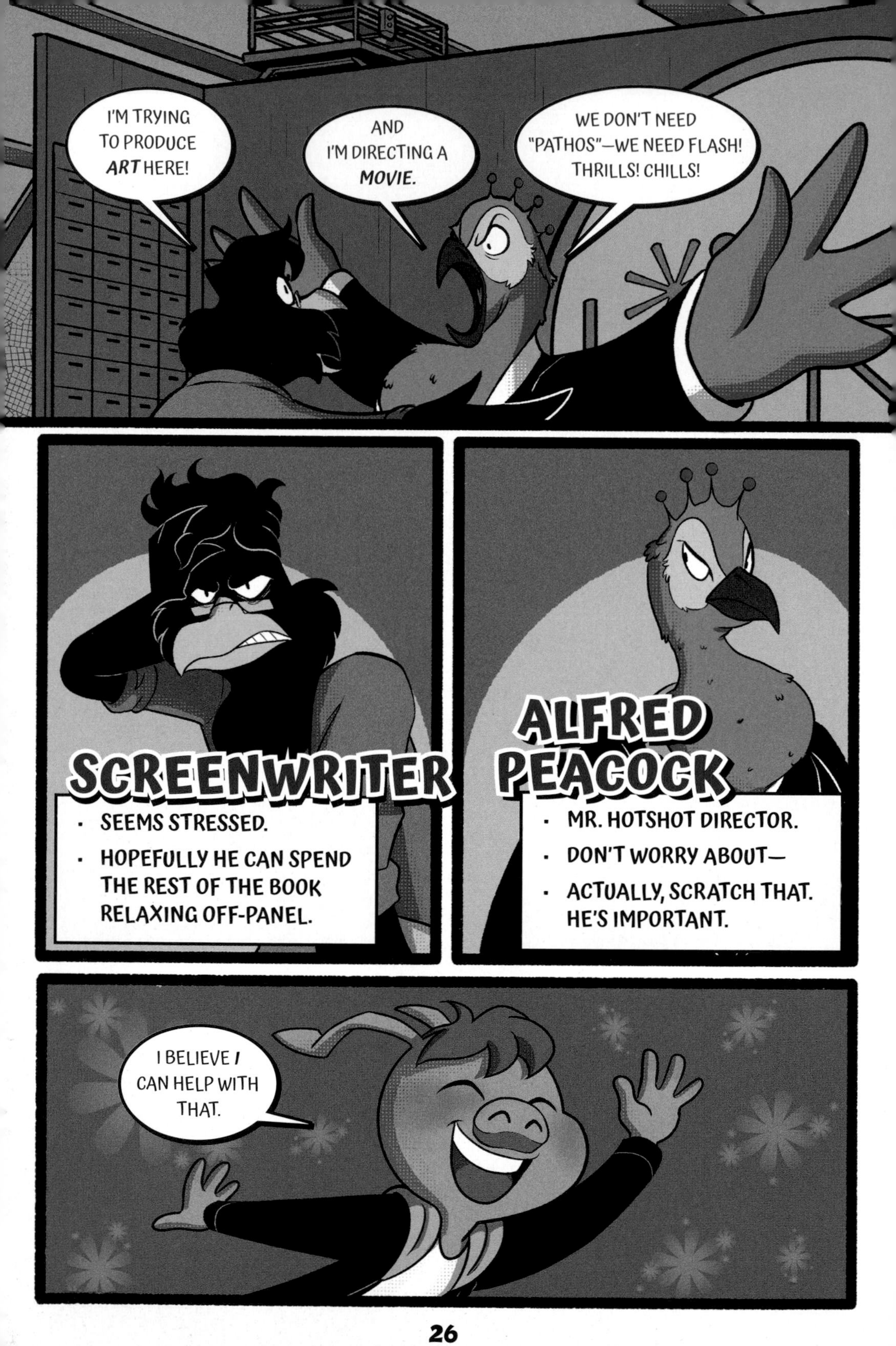
I'M TRYING TO PRODUCE **ART** HERE!
AND I'M DIRECTING A ***MOVIE.***
WE DON'T NEED "PATHOS"—WE NEED FLASH! THRILLS! CHILLS!
SCREENWRITER
· SEEMS STRESSED.
· HOPEFULLY HE CAN SPEND THE REST OF THE BOOK RELAXING OFF-PANEL.
ALFRED PEACOCK
· MR. HOTSHOT DIRECTOR.
· DON'T WORRY ABOUT—
· ACTUALLY, SCRATCH THAT. HE'S IMPORTANT.
I BELIEVE ***I*** CAN HELP WITH THAT.

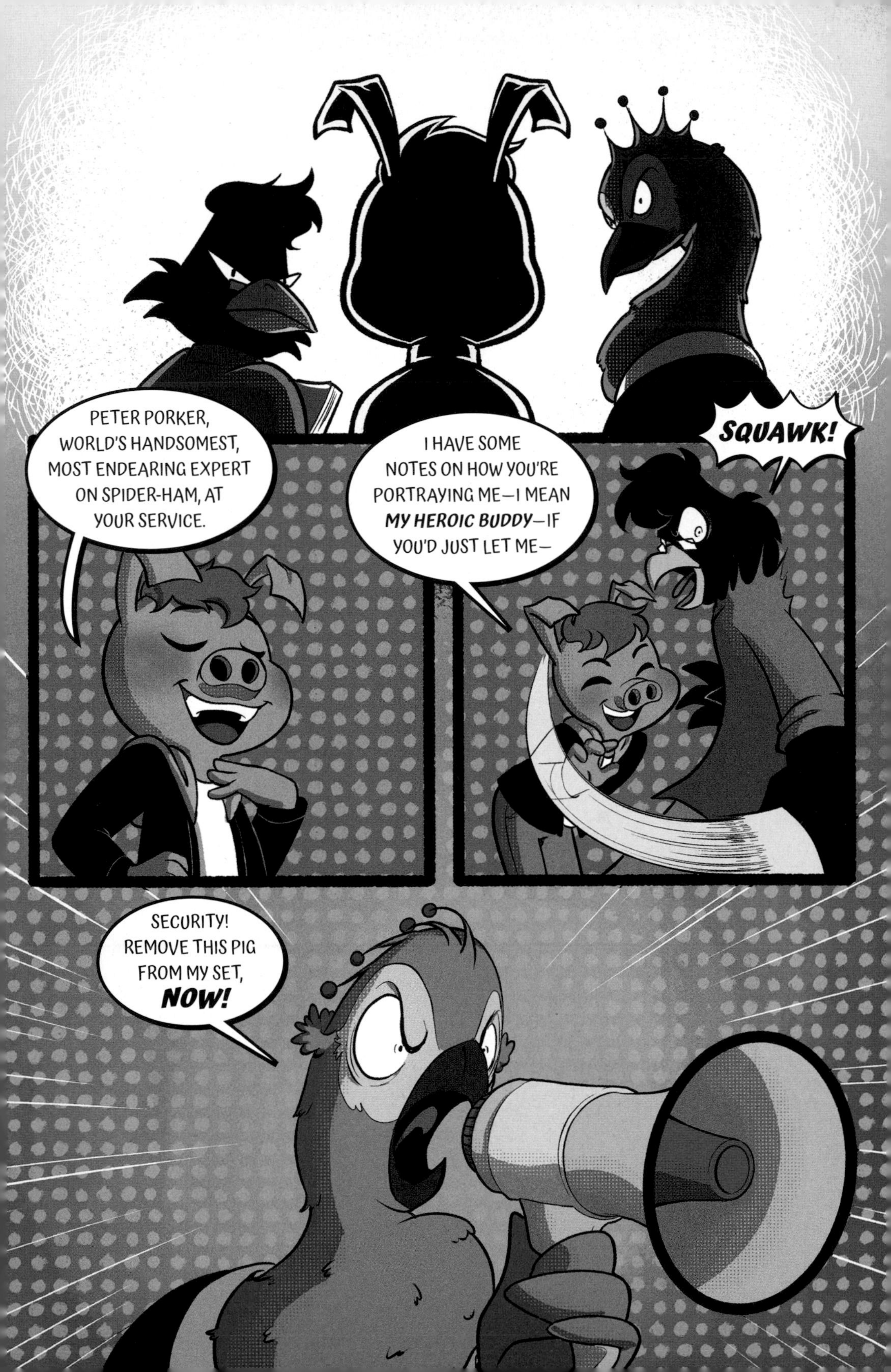
PETER PORKER, WORLD'S HANDSOMEST, MOST ENDEARING EXPERT ON SPIDER-HAM, AT YOUR SERVICE.
I HAVE SOME NOTES ON HOW YOU'RE PORTRAYING ME—I MEAN *MY HEROIC BUDDY*—IF YOU'D JUST LET ME—
SQUAWK!
SECURITY! REMOVE THIS PIG FROM MY SET, **NOW!**

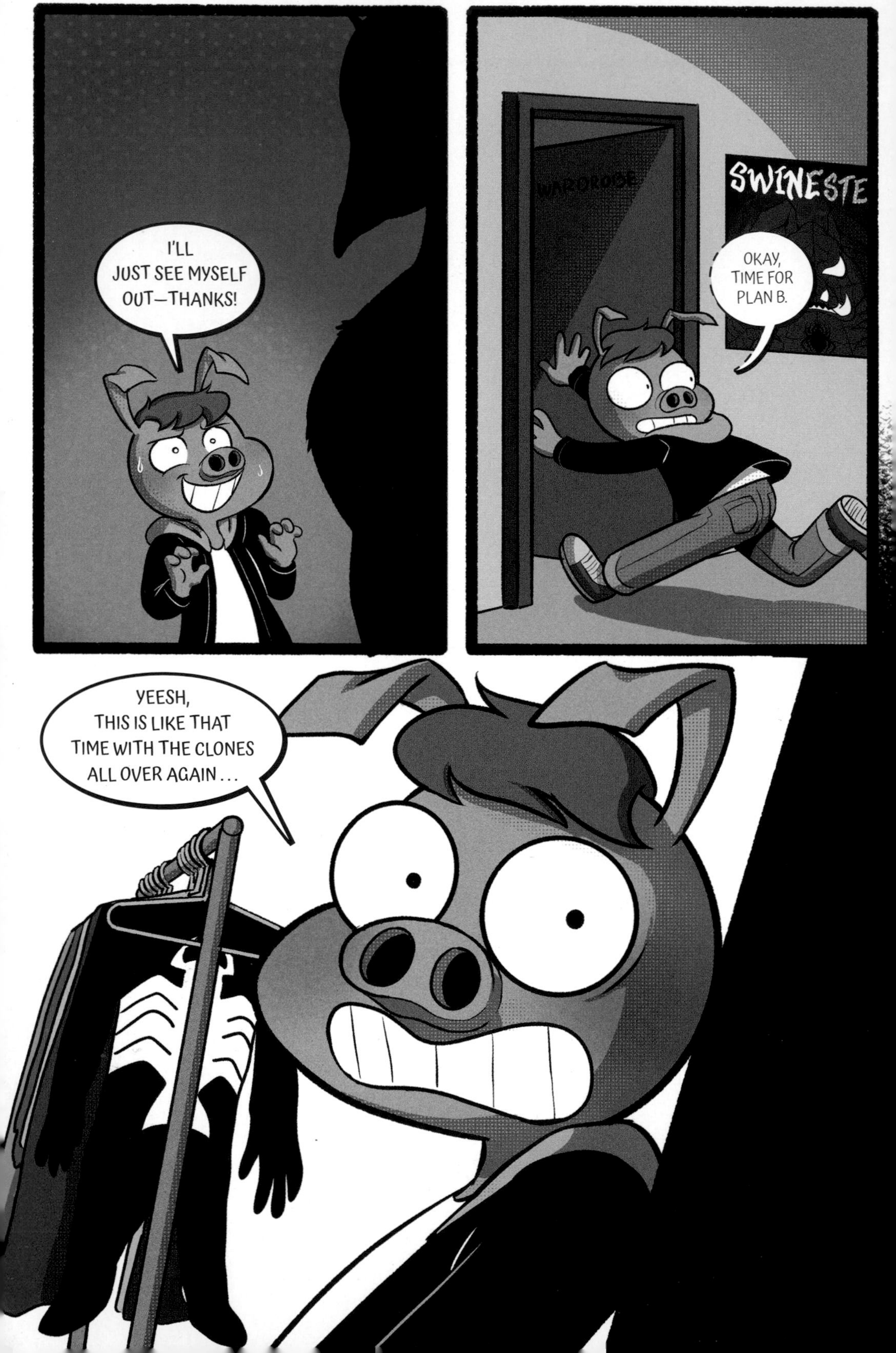
I'LL JUST SEE MYSELF OUT—THANKS!
WARDROBE
SWINESTE
OKAY, TIME FOR PLAN B.
YEESH, THIS IS LIKE THAT TIME WITH THE CLONES ALL OVER AGAIN . . .

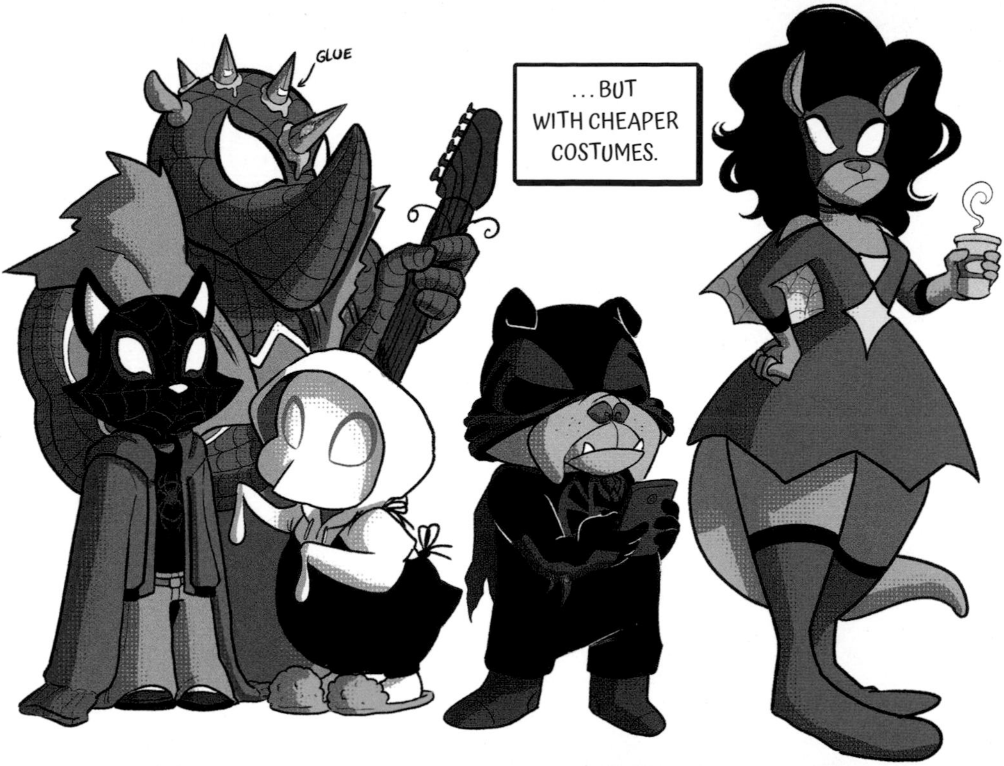
GLUE
. . . BUT
WITH CHEAPER
COSTUMES.

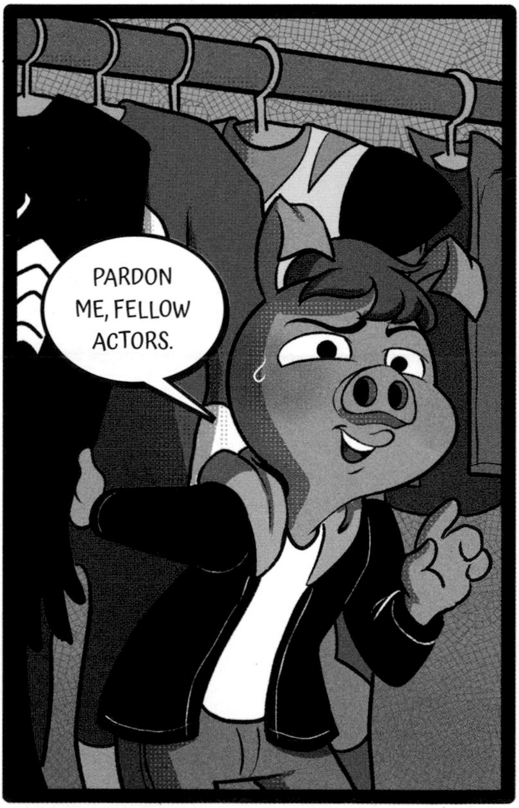
PARDON
ME, FELLOW
ACTORS.

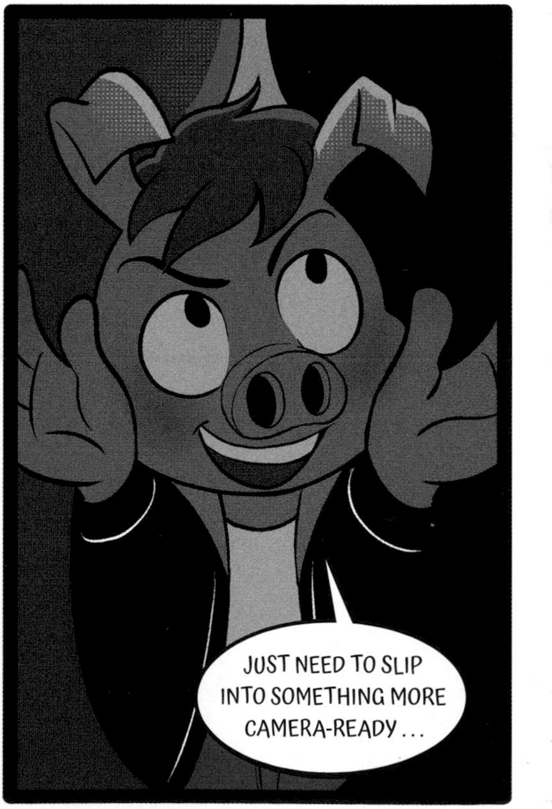
JUST NEED TO SLIP
INTO SOMETHING MORE
CAMERA-READY . . .

CHAPTER THREE:
BE-SWINED THE SCENES!

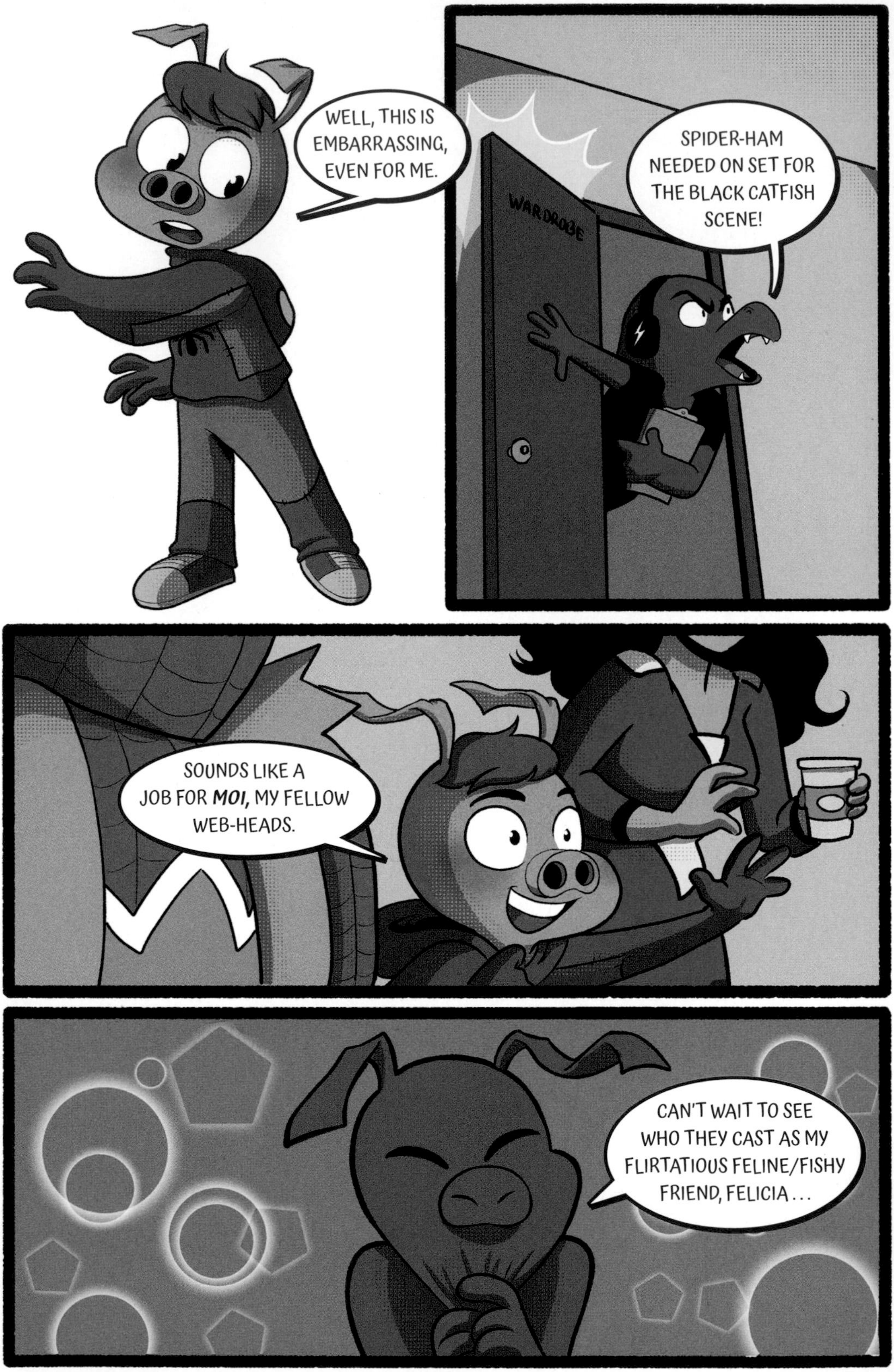
WELL, THIS IS EMBARRASSING, EVEN FOR ME.
SPIDER-HAM NEEDED ON SET FOR THE BLACK CATFISH SCENE!
WARDROBE
SOUNDS LIKE A JOB FOR **MOI**, MY FELLOW WEB-HEADS.
CAN'T WAIT TO SEE WHO THEY CAST AS MY FLIRTATIOUS FELINE/FISHY FRIEND, FELICIA . . .

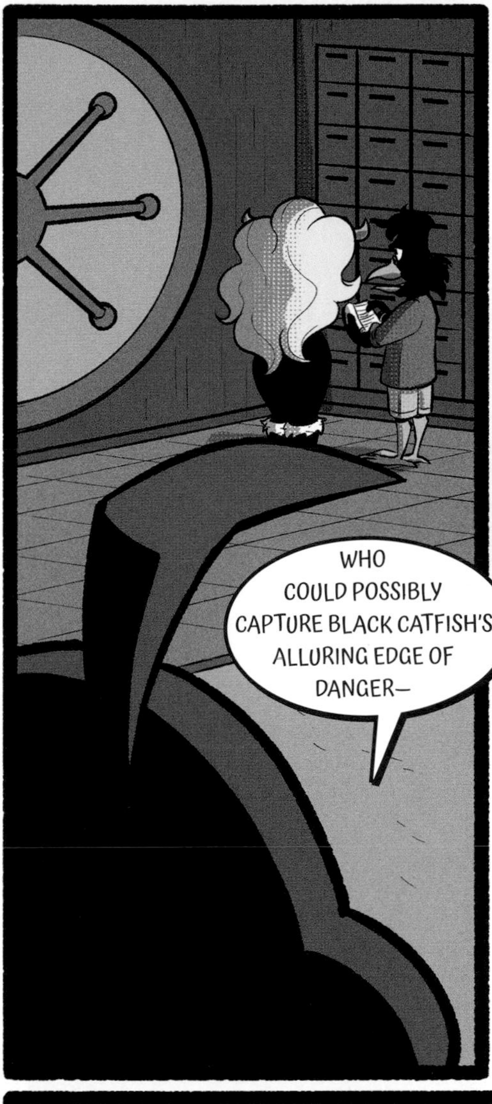
WHO COULD POSSIBLY CAPTURE BLACK CATFISH'S ALLURING EDGE OF DANGER—

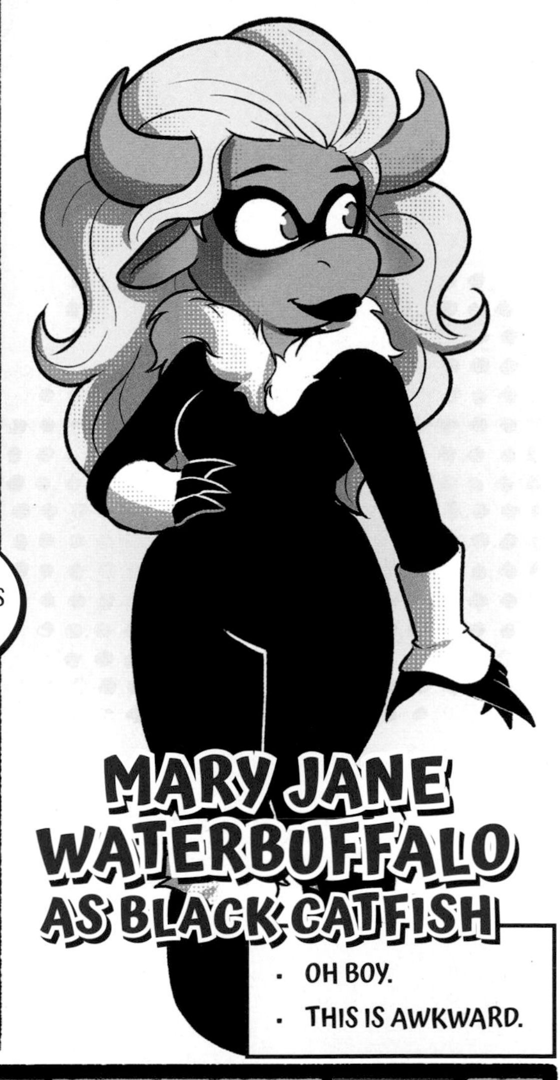
MARY JANE WATERBUFFALO AS BLACK CATFISH
• OH BOY.
• THIS IS AWKWARD.

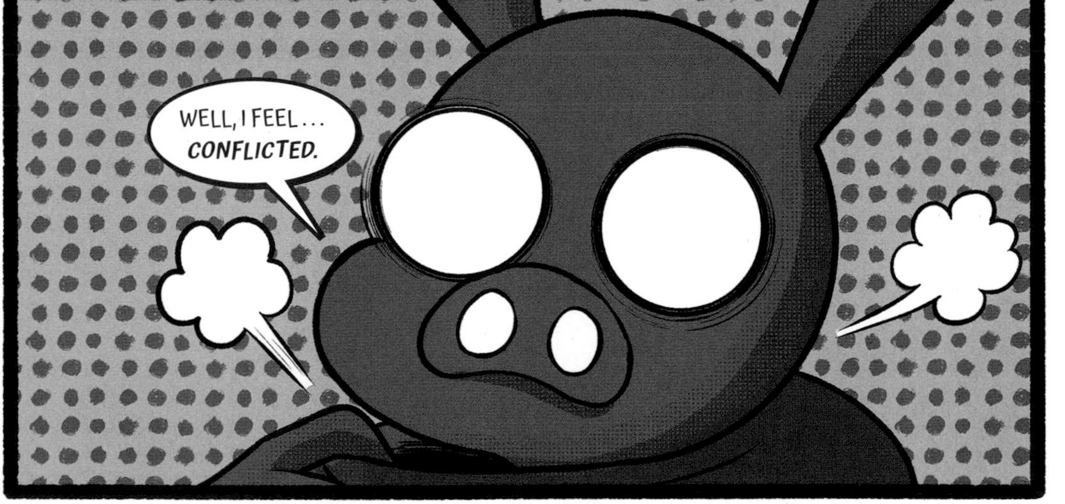
WELL, I FEEL . . . CONFLICTED.

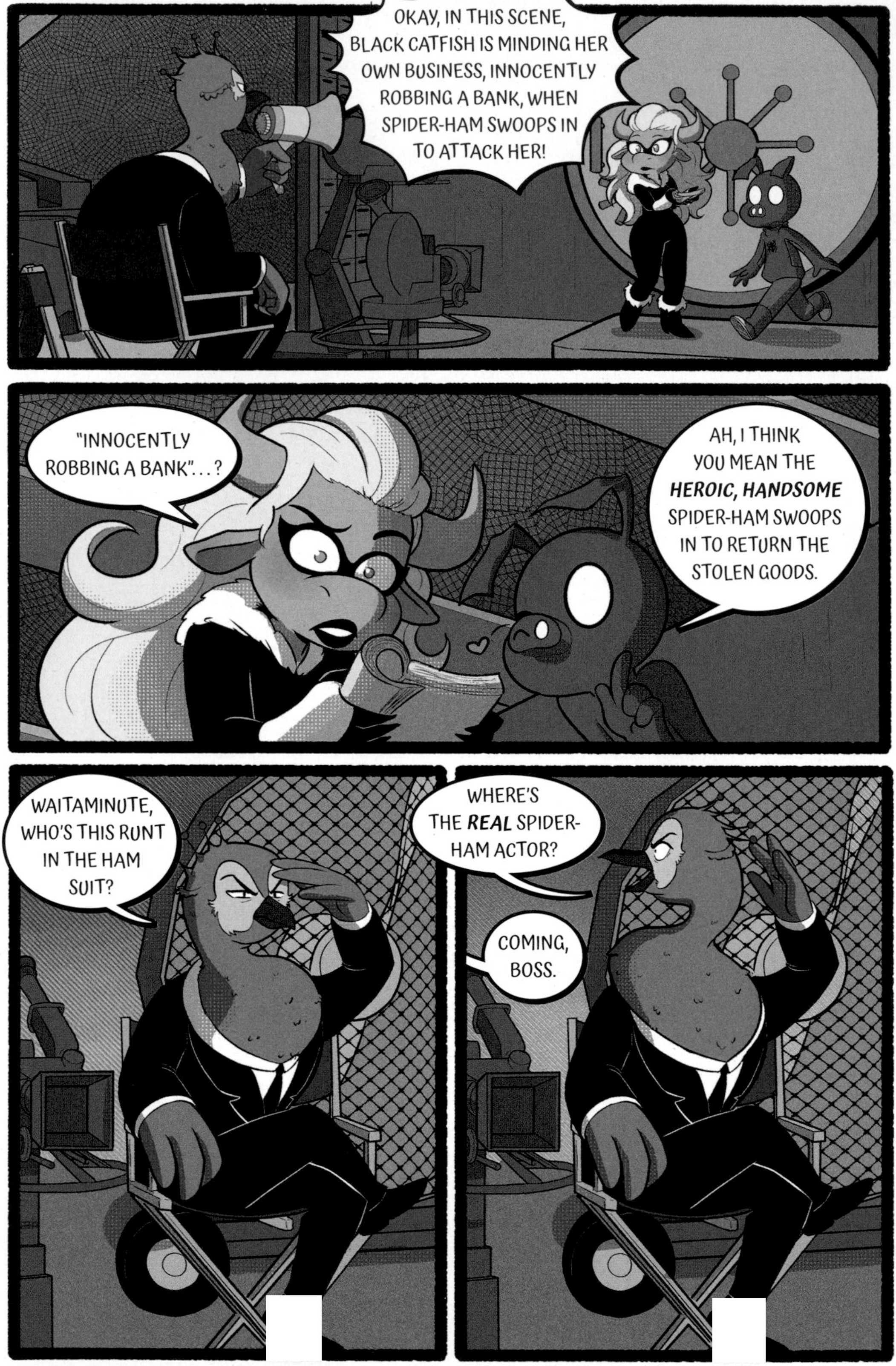
OKAY, IN THIS SCENE, BLACK CATFISH IS MINDING HER OWN BUSINESS, INNOCENTLY ROBBING A BANK, WHEN SPIDER-HAM SWOOPS IN TO ATTACK HER!
"INNOCENTLY ROBBING A BANK"...?
AH, I THINK YOU MEAN THE **HEROIC, HANDSOME** SPIDER-HAM SWOOPS IN TO RETURN THE STOLEN GOODS.
WAITAMINUTE, WHO'S THIS RUNT IN THE HAM SUIT?
WHERE'S THE **REAL** SPIDER-HAM ACTOR?
COMING, BOSS.

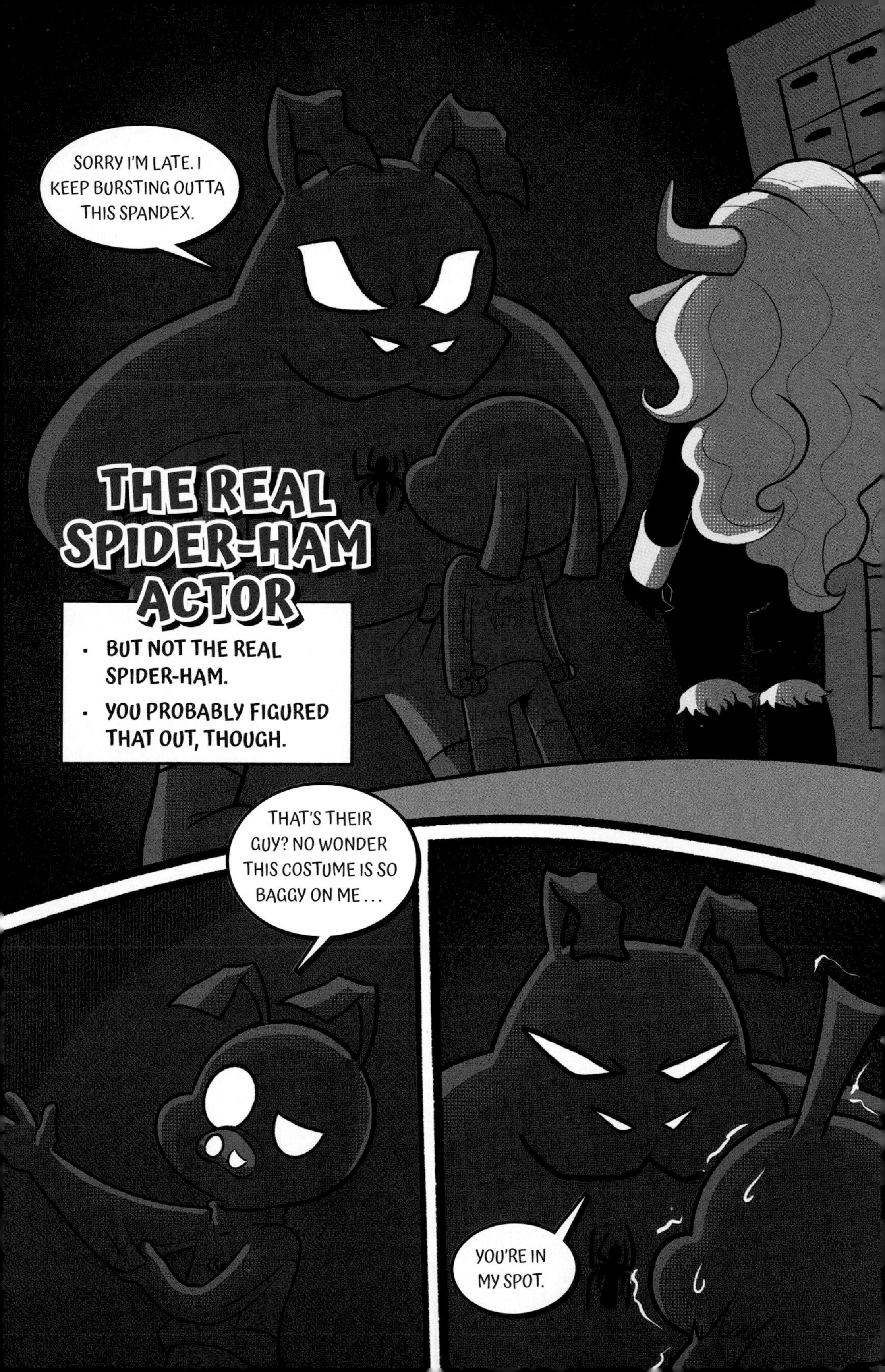
SORRY I'M LATE. I KEEP BURSTING OUTTA THIS SPANDEX.
THE REAL SPIDER-HAM ACTOR
• BUT NOT THE REAL SPIDER-HAM.
• YOU PROBABLY FIGURED THAT OUT, THOUGH.
THAT'S THEIR GUY? NO WONDER THIS COSTUME IS SO BAGGY ON ME . . .
YOU'RE IN MY SPOT.

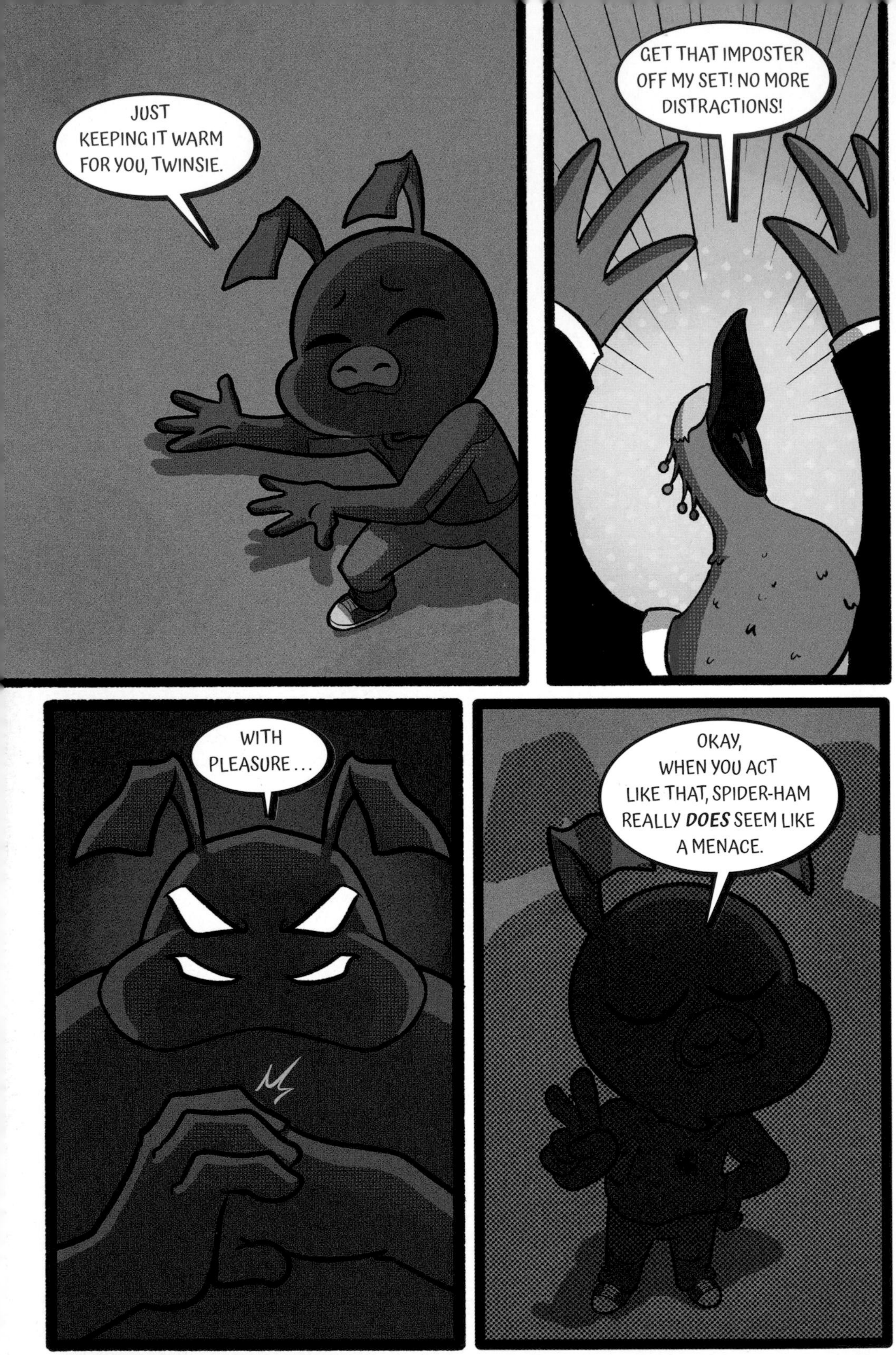
JUST KEEPING IT WARM FOR YOU, TWINSIE.
GET THAT IMPOSTER OFF MY SET! NO MORE DISTRACTIONS!
WITH PLEASURE . . .
OKAY, WHEN YOU ACT LIKE THAT, SPIDER-HAM REALLY **DOES** SEEM LIKE A MENACE.

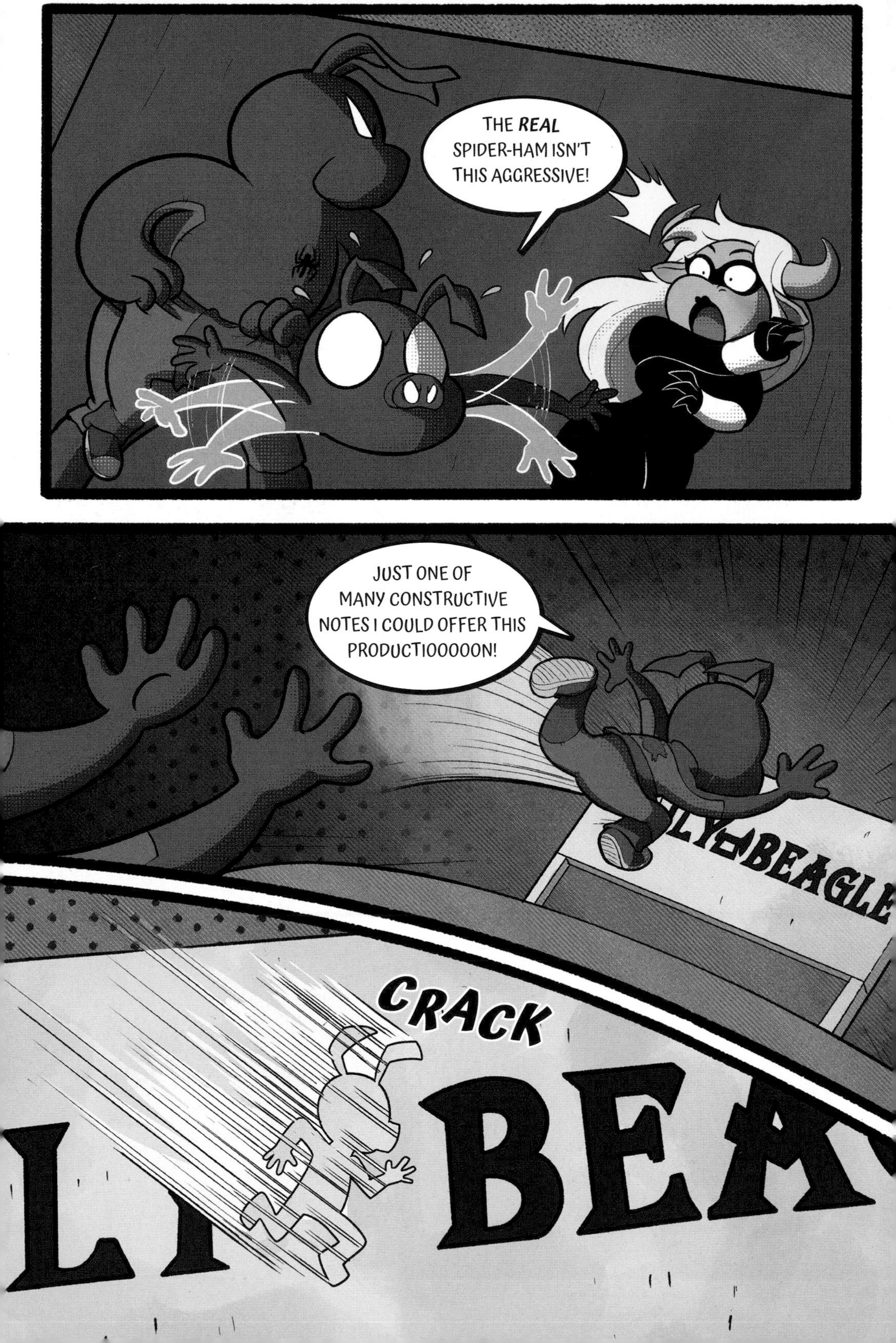
THE *REAL* SPIDER-HAM ISN'T THIS AGGRESSIVE!
JUST ONE OF MANY CONSTRUCTIVE NOTES I COULD OFFER THIS PRODUCTIOOOOON!
BEAGLE
CRACK

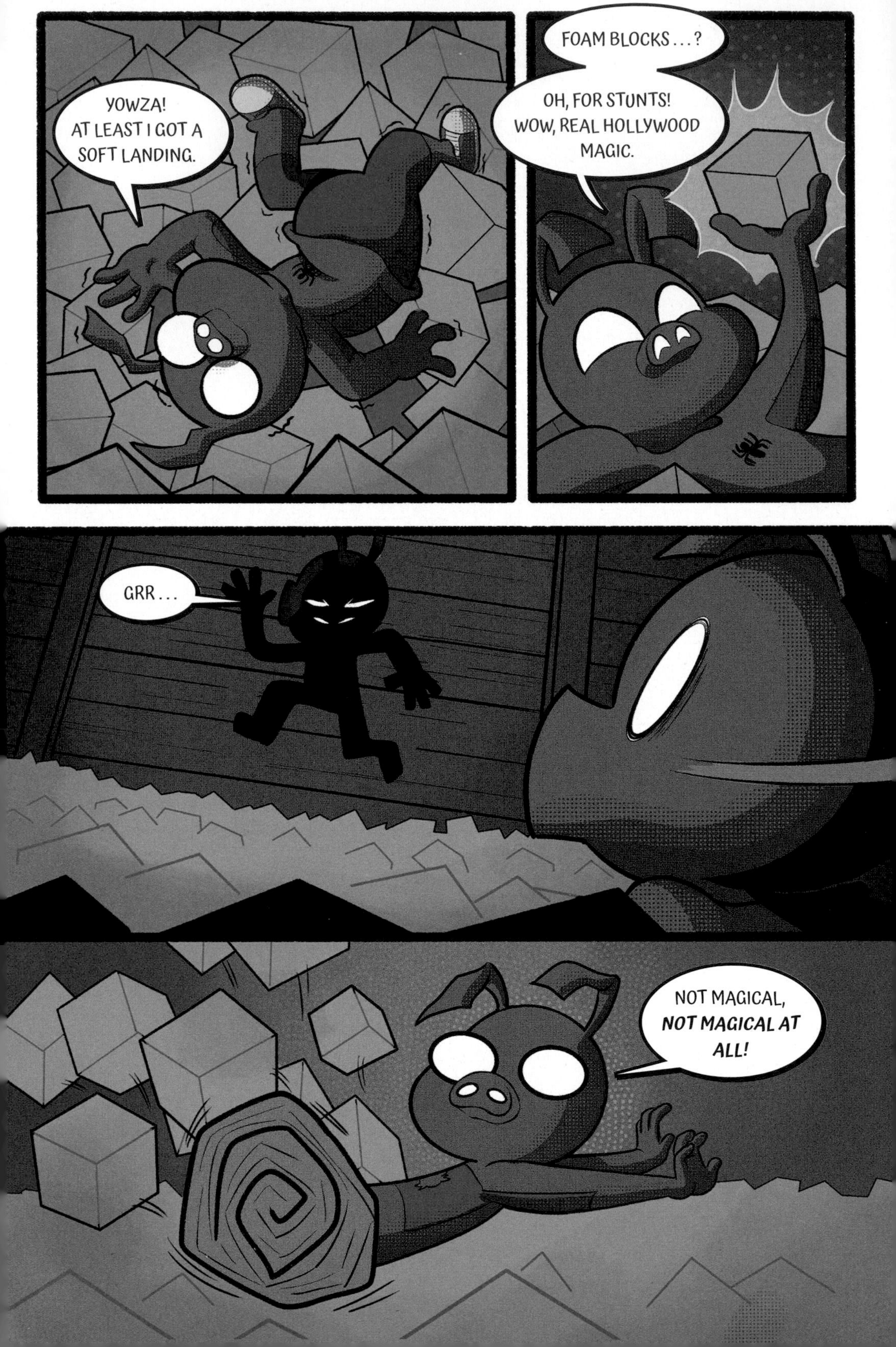
YOWZA!
AT LEAST I GOT A SOFT LANDING.
FOAM BLOCKS . . . ?
OH, FOR STUNTS! WOW, REAL HOLLYWOOD MAGIC.
GRR . . .
NOT MAGICAL, **NOT MAGICAL AT ALL!**

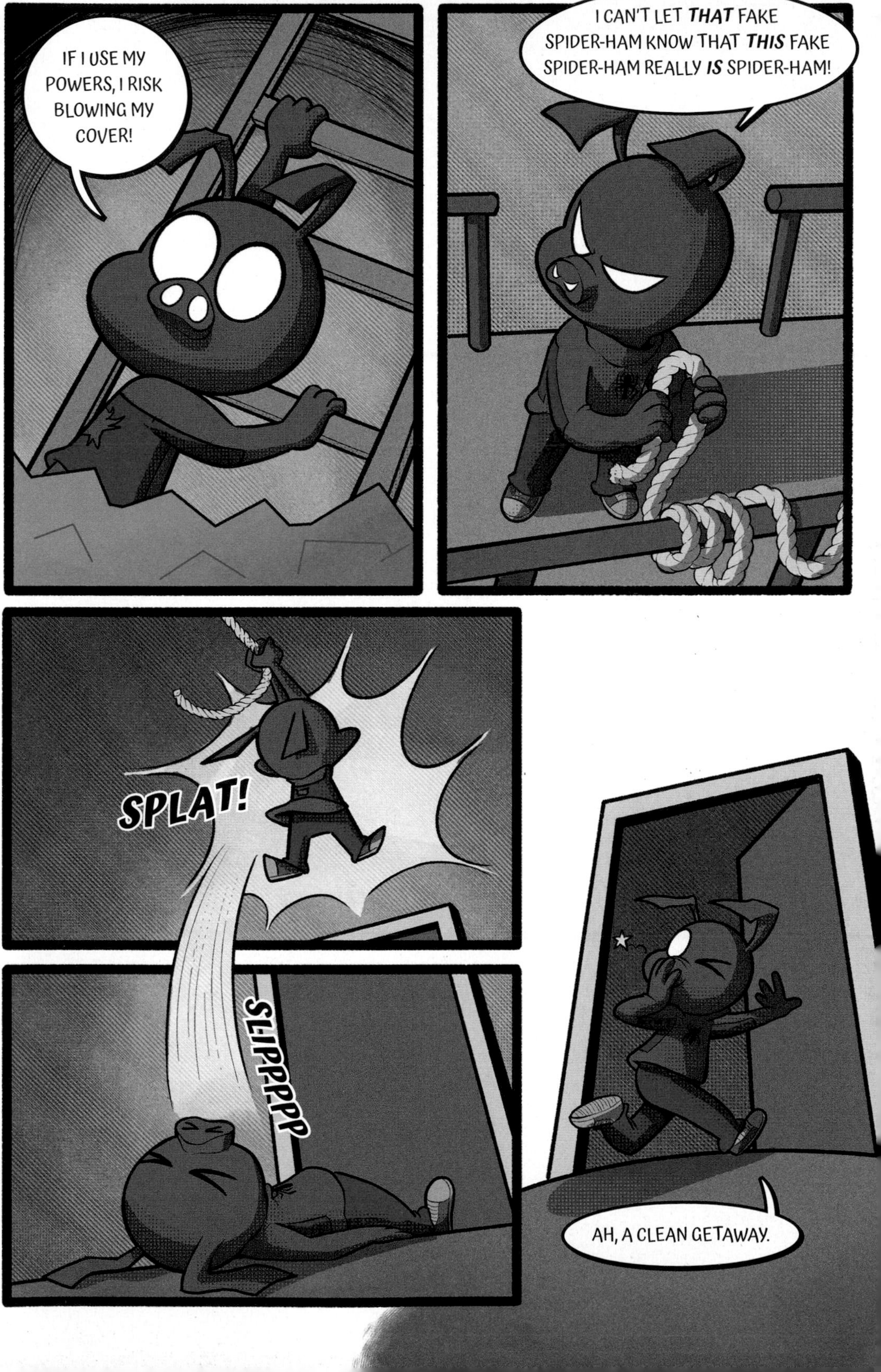
IF I USE MY POWERS, I RISK BLOWING MY COVER!
I CAN'T LET THAT FAKE SPIDER-HAM KNOW THAT THIS FAKE SPIDER-HAM REALLY IS SPIDER-HAM!
SPLAT!
SLIPPPPP
AH, A CLEAN GETAWAY.

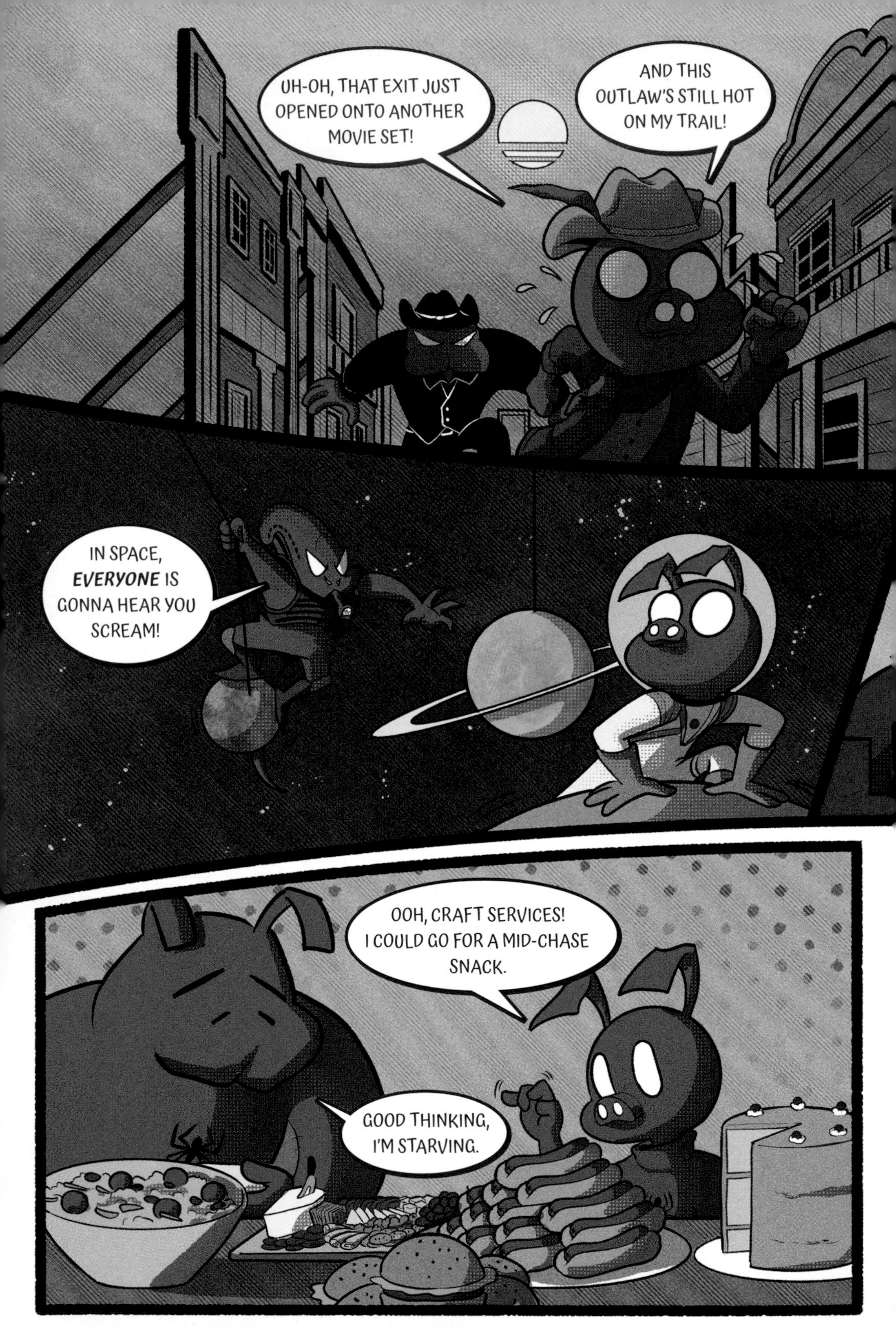
UH-OH, THAT EXIT JUST OPENED ONTO ANOTHER MOVIE SET!
AND THIS OUTLAW'S STILL HOT ON MY TRAIL!
IN SPACE, EVERYONE IS GONNA HEAR YOU SCREAM!
OOH, CRAFT SERVICES! I COULD GO FOR A MID-CHASE SNACK.
GOOD THINKING, I'M STARVING.

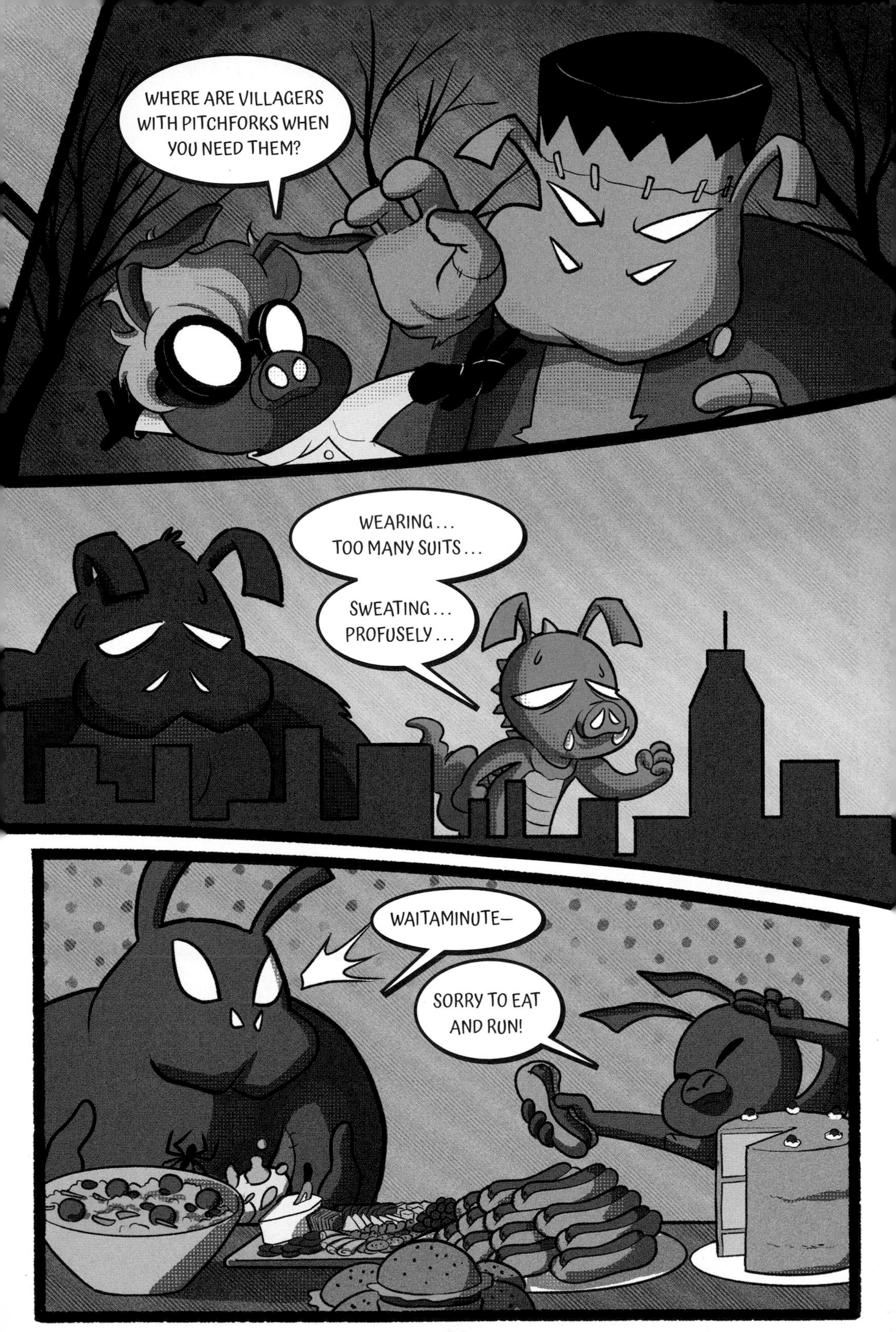
WHERE ARE VILLAGERS WITH PITCHFORKS WHEN YOU NEED THEM?
WEARING... TOO MANY SUITS...
SWEATING... PROFUSELY...
WAITAMINUTE—
SORRY TO EAT AND RUN!

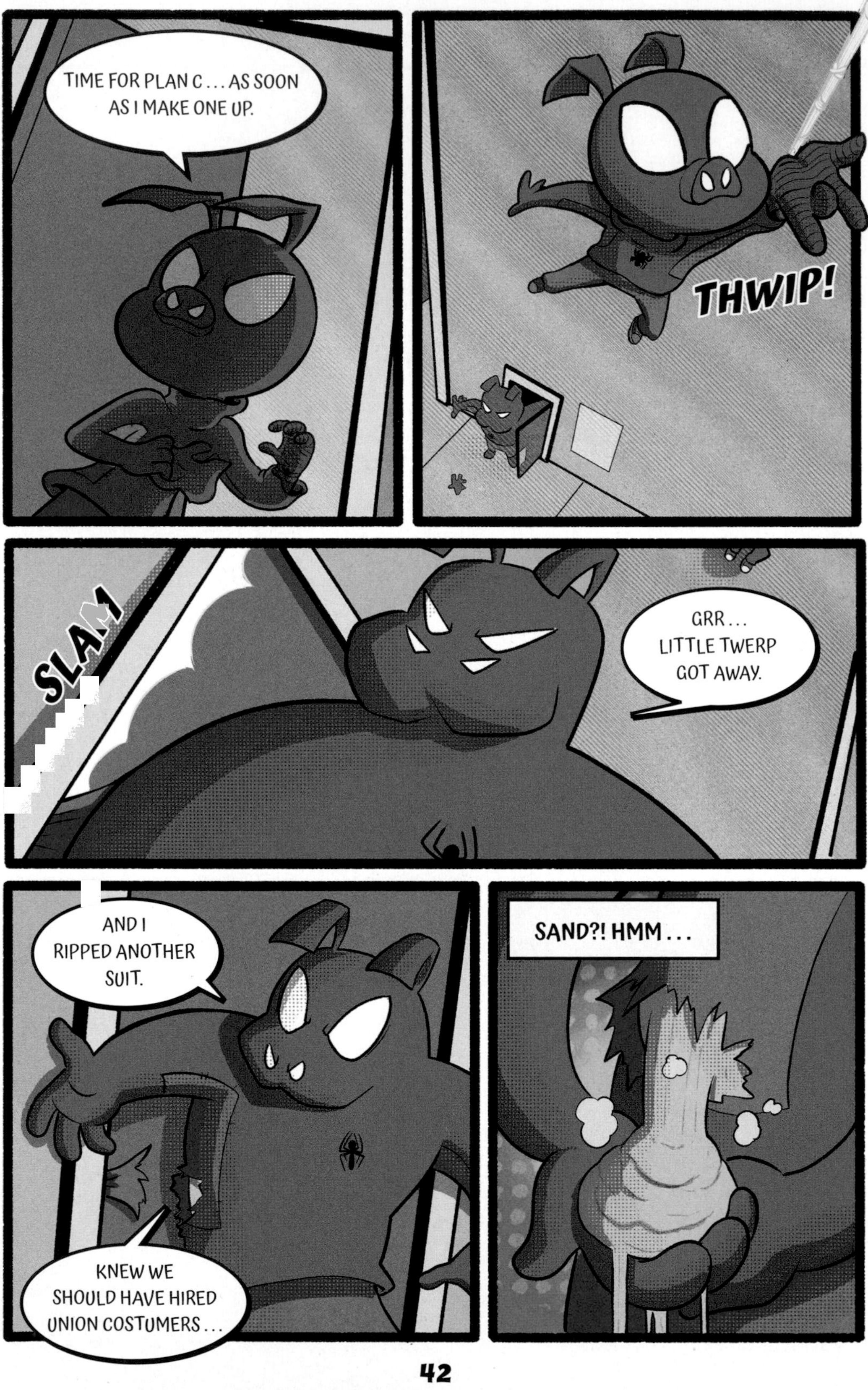
TIME FOR PLAN C . . . AS SOON AS I MAKE ONE UP.
THWIP!
SLAM
GRR . . . LITTLE TWERP GOT AWAY.
AND I RIPPED ANOTHER SUIT.
KNEW WE SHOULD HAVE HIRED UNION COSTUMERS . . .
SAND?! HMM . . .

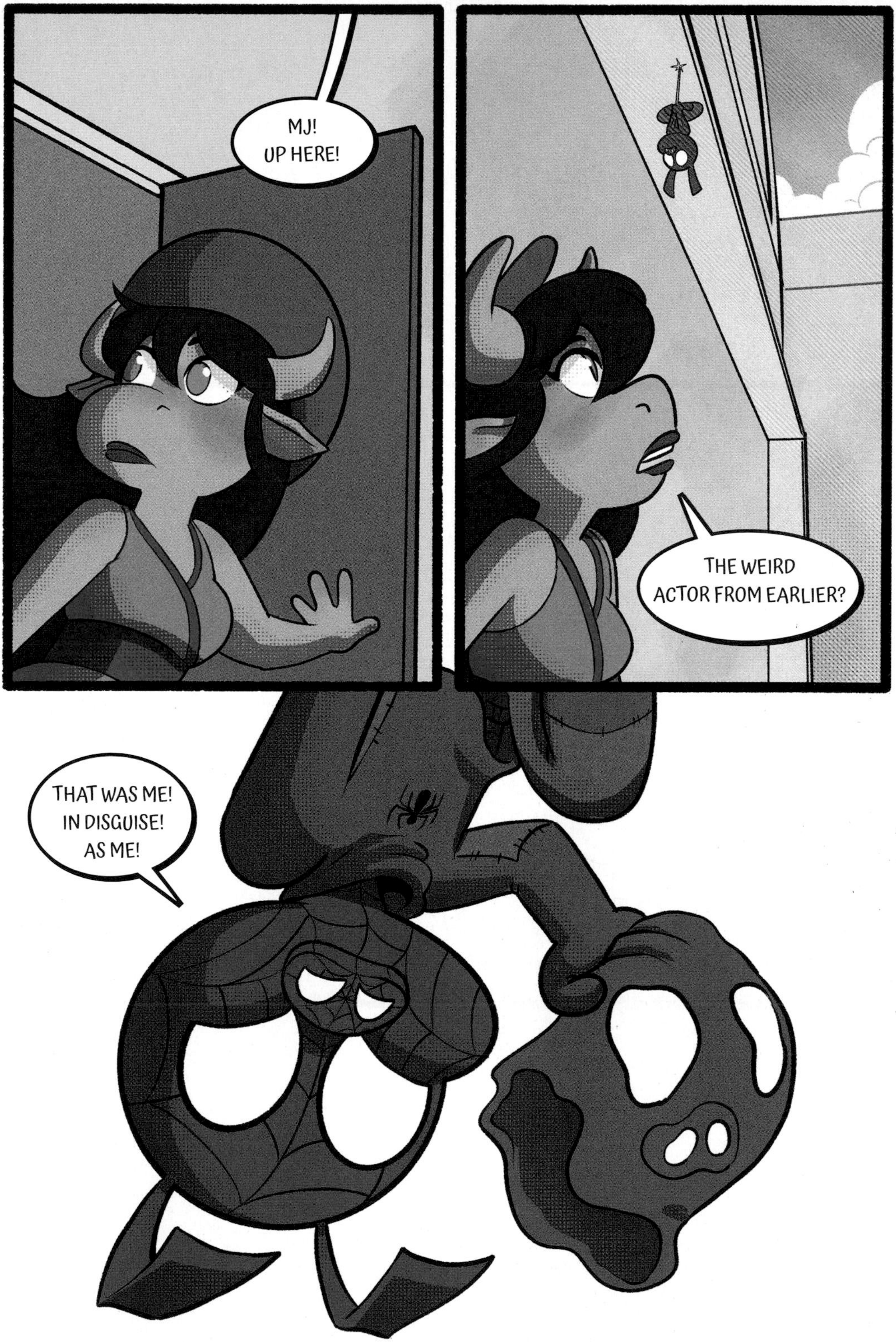
MJ!
UP HERE!
THE WEIRD ACTOR FROM EARLIER?
THAT WAS ME! IN DISGUISE! AS ME!

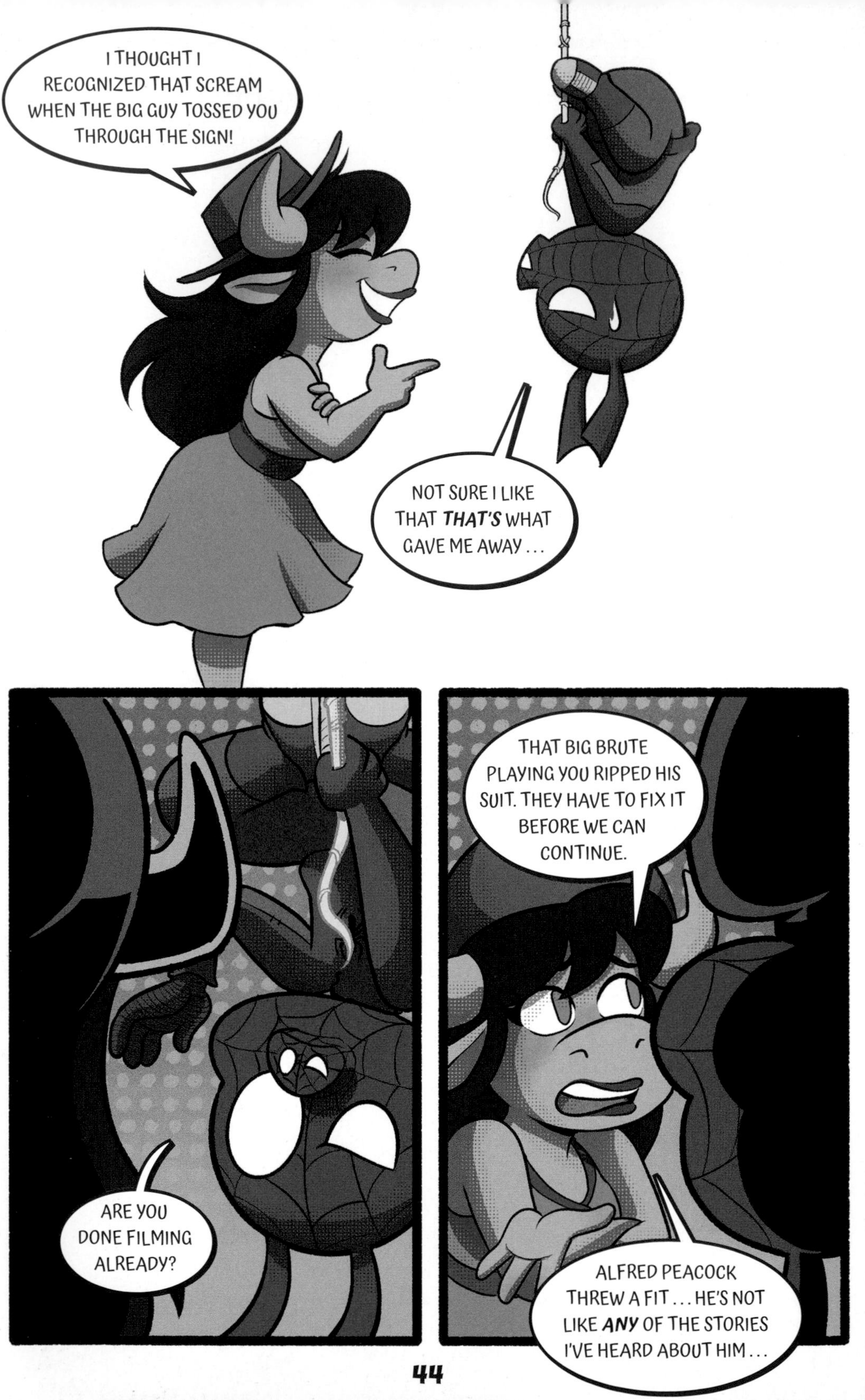
I THOUGHT I RECOGNIZED THAT SCREAM WHEN THE BIG GUY TOSSED YOU THROUGH THE SIGN!
NOT SURE I LIKE THAT ***THAT'S*** WHAT GAVE ME AWAY . . .
ARE YOU DONE FILMING ALREADY?
THAT BIG BRUTE PLAYING YOU RIPPED HIS SUIT. THEY HAVE TO FIX IT BEFORE WE CAN CONTINUE.
ALFRED PEACOCK THREW A FIT . . . HE'S NOT LIKE ***ANY*** OF THE STORIES I'VE HEARD ABOUT HIM . . .

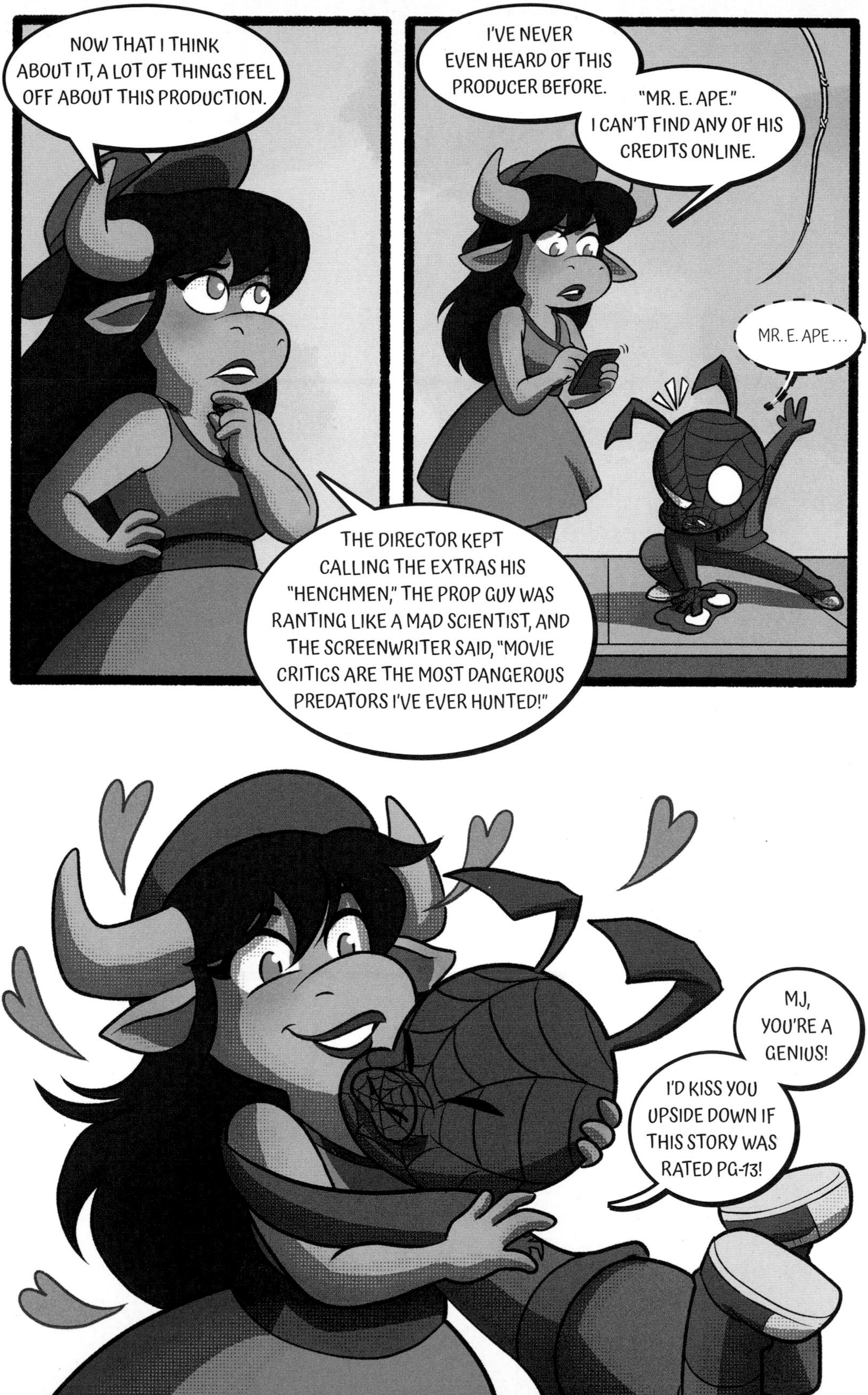
NOW THAT I THINK ABOUT IT, A LOT OF THINGS FEEL OFF ABOUT THIS PRODUCTION.
I'VE NEVER EVEN HEARD OF THIS PRODUCER BEFORE.
"MR. E. APE." I CAN'T FIND ANY OF HIS CREDITS ONLINE.
MR. E. APE...
THE DIRECTOR KEPT CALLING THE EXTRAS HIS "HENCHMEN," THE PROP GUY WAS RANTING LIKE A MAD SCIENTIST, AND THE SCREENWRITER SAID, "MOVIE CRITICS ARE THE MOST DANGEROUS PREDATORS I'VE EVER HUNTED!"
MJ, YOU'RE A GENIUS!
I'D KISS YOU UPSIDE DOWN IF THIS STORY WAS RATED PG-13!

CHAPTER FOUR:
THE PIG
REVEAL!

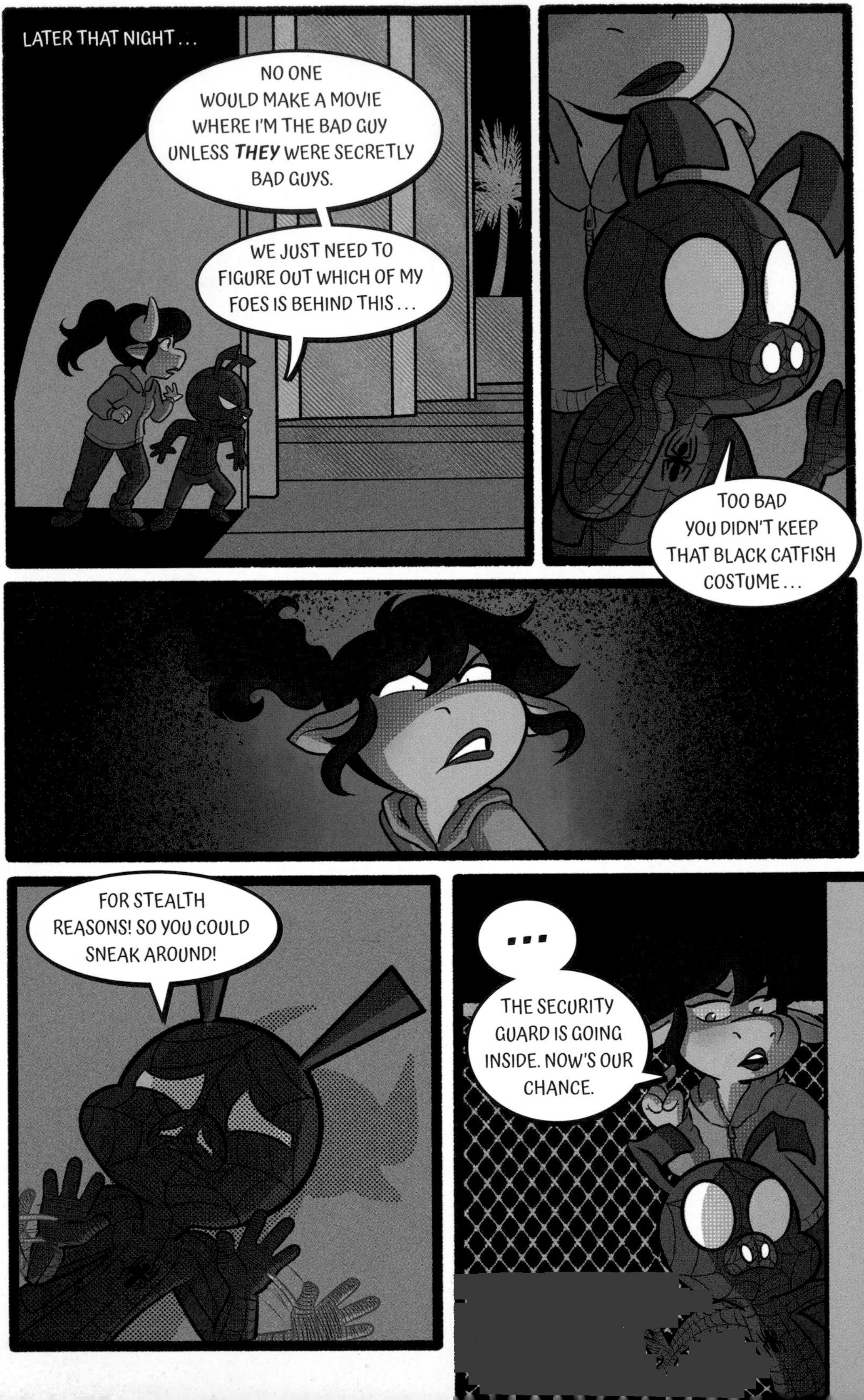
LATER THAT NIGHT . . .
NO ONE WOULD MAKE A MOVIE WHERE I'M THE BAD GUY UNLESS *THEY* WERE SECRETLY BAD GUYS.
WE JUST NEED TO FIGURE OUT WHICH OF MY FOES IS BEHIND THIS . . .
TOO BAD YOU DIDN'T KEEP THAT BLACK CATFISH COSTUME . . .
FOR STEALTH REASONS! SO YOU COULD SNEAK AROUND!
...
THE SECURITY GUARD IS GOING INSIDE. NOW'S OUR CHANCE.
[redacted]

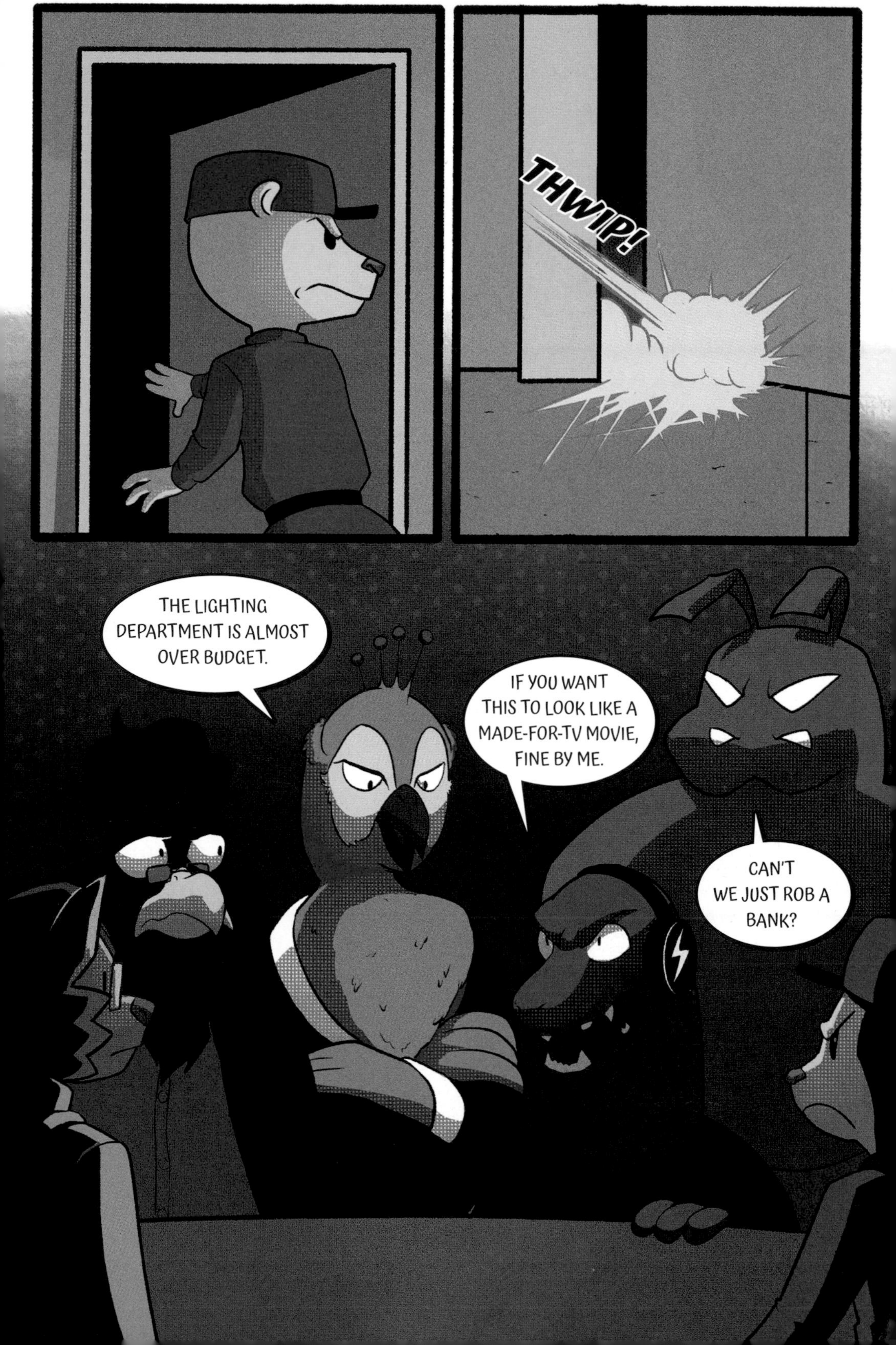
THWIP!
THE LIGHTING DEPARTMENT IS ALMOST OVER BUDGET.
IF YOU WANT THIS TO LOOK LIKE A MADE-FOR-TV MOVIE, FINE BY ME.
CAN'T WE JUST ROB A BANK?

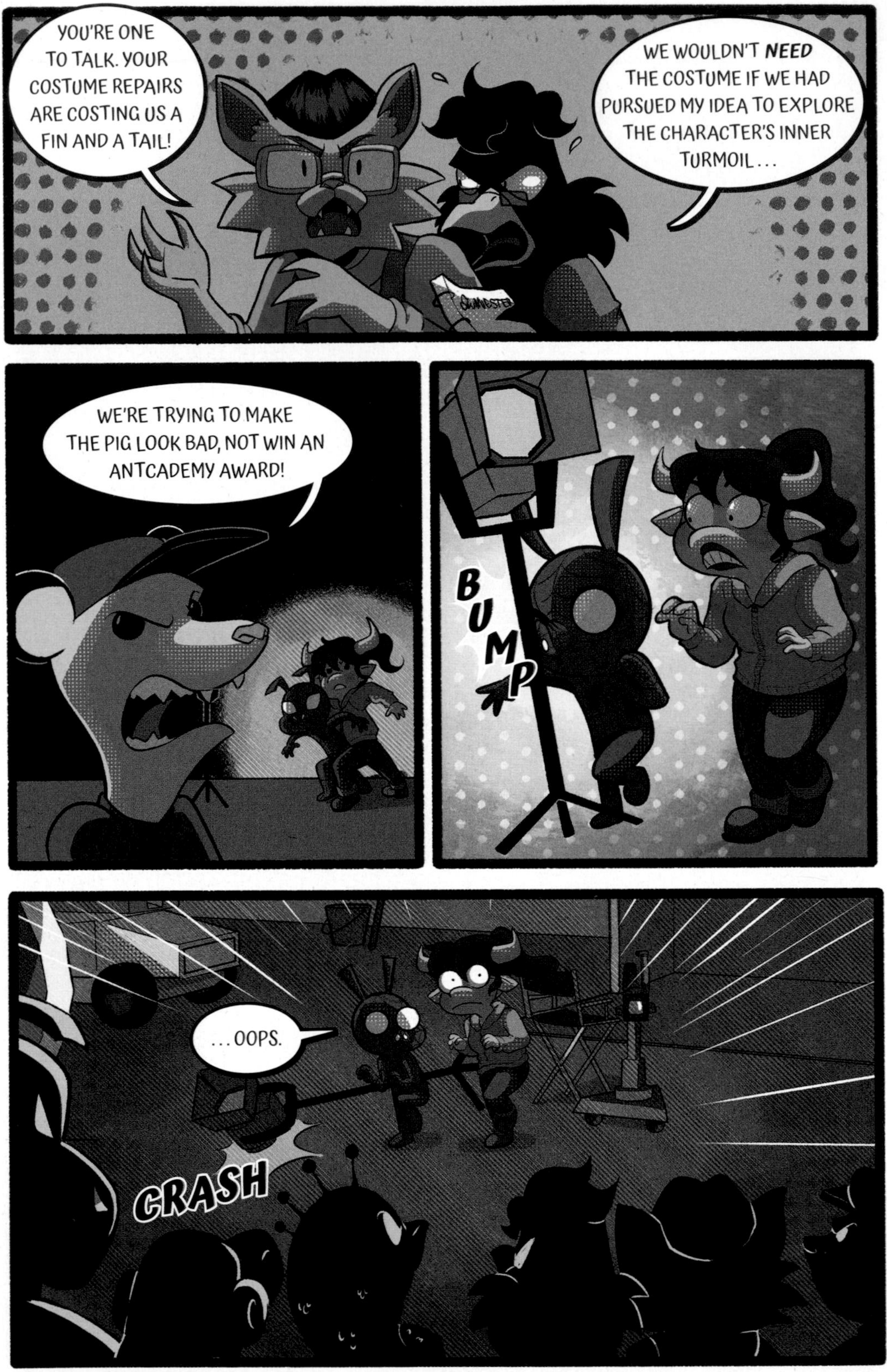
YOU'RE ONE TO TALK. YOUR COSTUME REPAIRS ARE COSTING US A FIN AND A TAIL!
WE WOULDN'T **NEED** THE COSTUME IF WE HAD PURSUED MY IDEA TO EXPLORE THE CHARACTER'S INNER TURMOIL...
WE'RE TRYING TO MAKE THE PIG LOOK BAD, NOT WIN AN ANTCADEMY AWARD!
BUMP
...OOPS.
CRASH

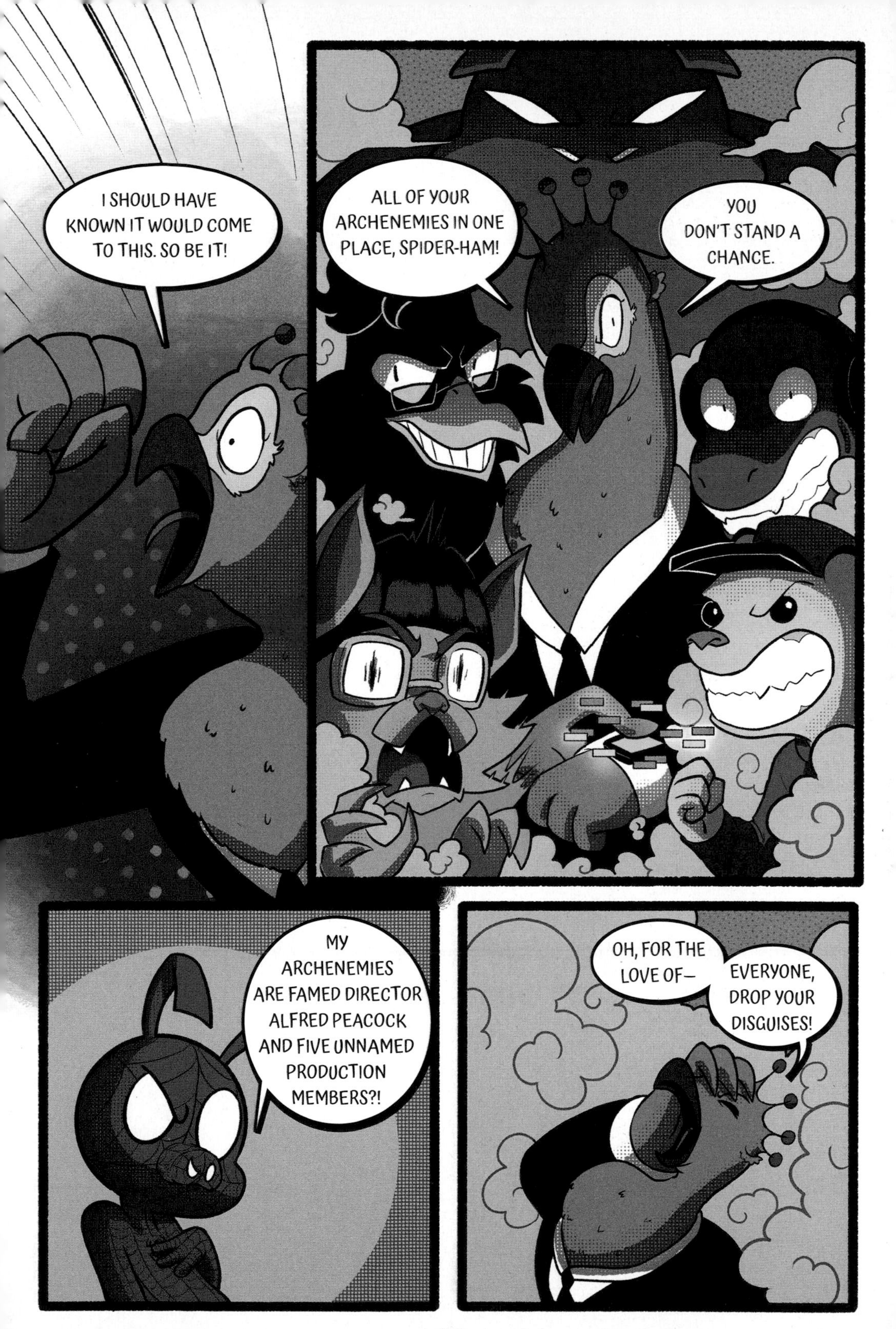
I SHOULD HAVE KNOWN IT WOULD COME TO THIS. SO BE IT!
ALL OF YOUR ARCHENEMIES IN ONE PLACE, SPIDER-HAM!
YOU DON'T STAND A CHANCE.
MY ARCHENEMIES ARE FAMED DIRECTOR ALFRED PEACOCK AND FIVE UNNAMED PRODUCTION MEMBERS?!
OH, FOR THE LOVE OF—
EVERYONE, DROP YOUR DISGUISES!

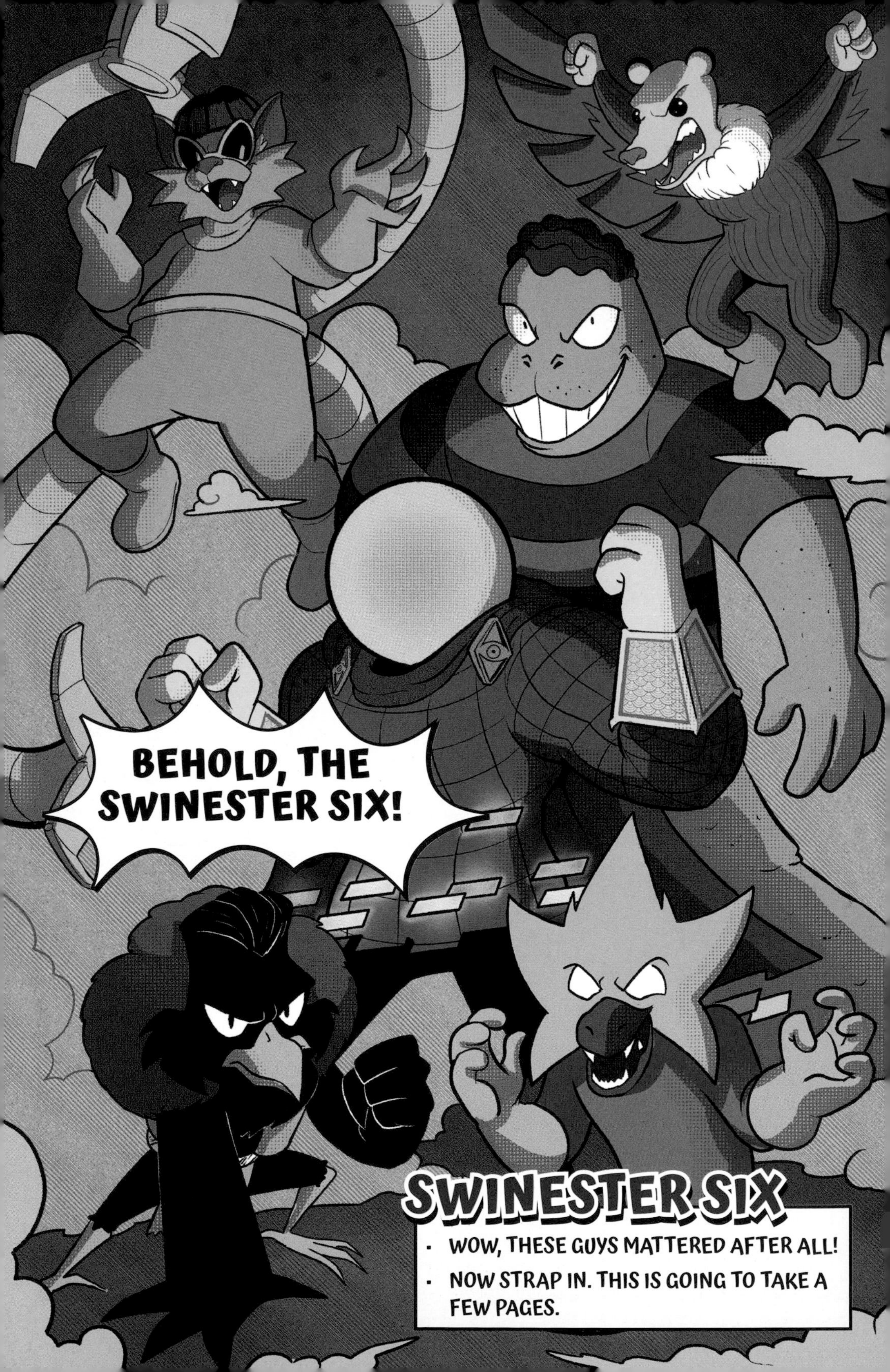
BEHOLD, THE SWINESTER SIX!
SWINESTER SIX
- WOW, THESE GUYS MATTERED AFTER ALL!
- NOW STRAP IN. THIS IS GOING TO TAKE A FEW PAGES.

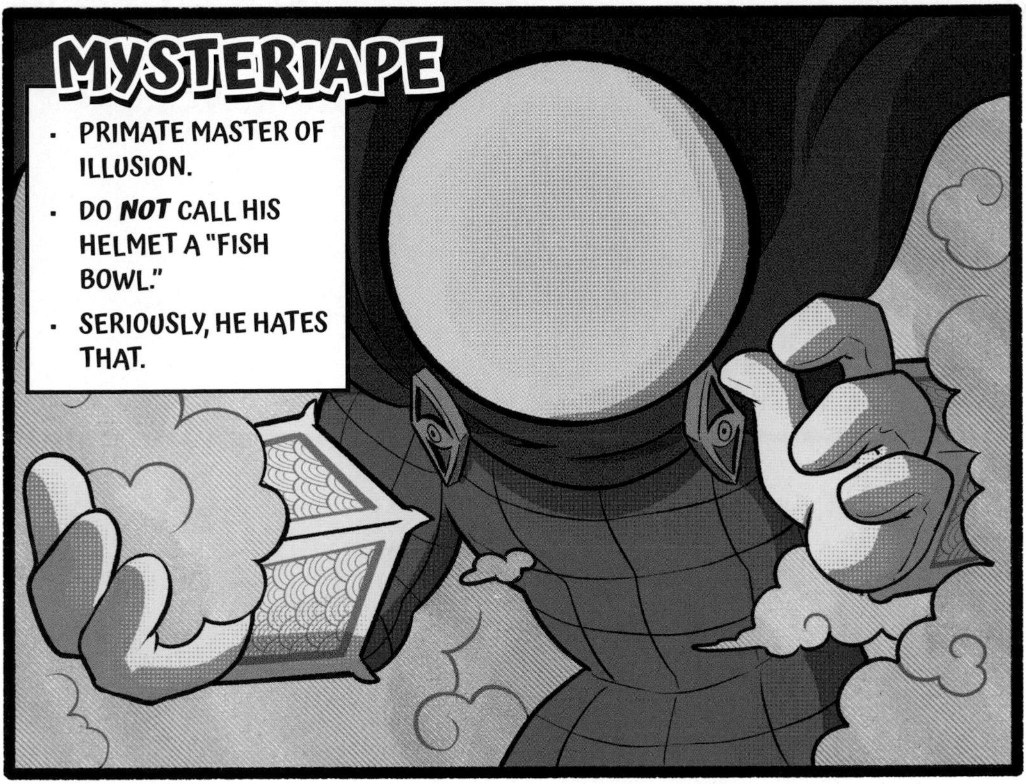
MYSTERIAPE
- PRIMATE MASTER OF ILLUSION.
- DO ***NOT*** CALL HIS HELMET A "FISH BOWL."
- SERIOUSLY, HE HATES THAT.

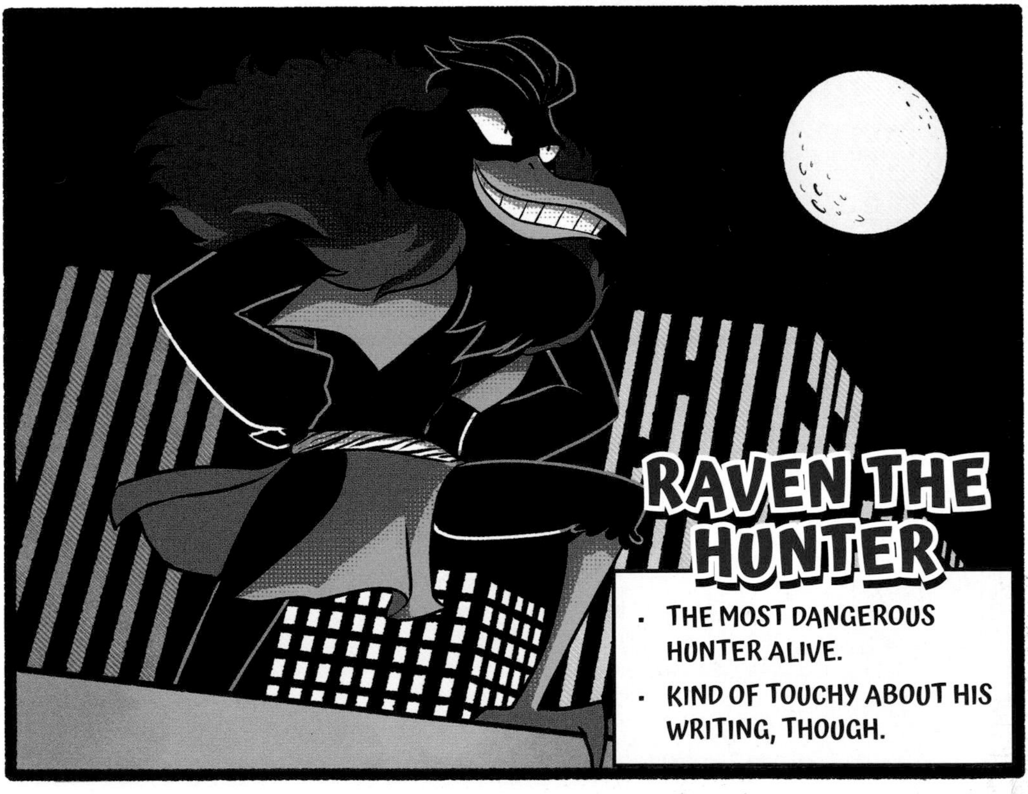
RAVEN THE HUNTER
- THE MOST DANGEROUS HUNTER ALIVE.
- KIND OF TOUCHY ABOUT HIS WRITING, THOUGH.

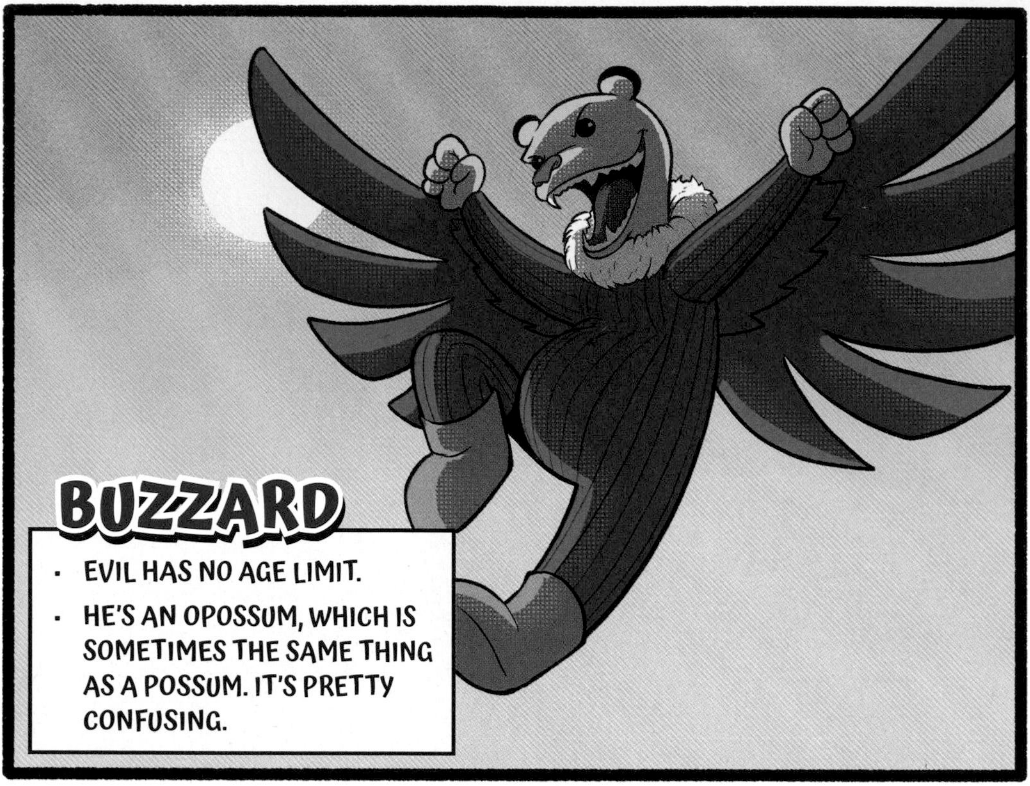
BUZZARD
• EVIL HAS NO AGE LIMIT.
• HE'S AN OPOSSUM, WHICH IS SOMETIMES THE SAME THING AS A POSSUM. IT'S PRETTY CONFUSING.

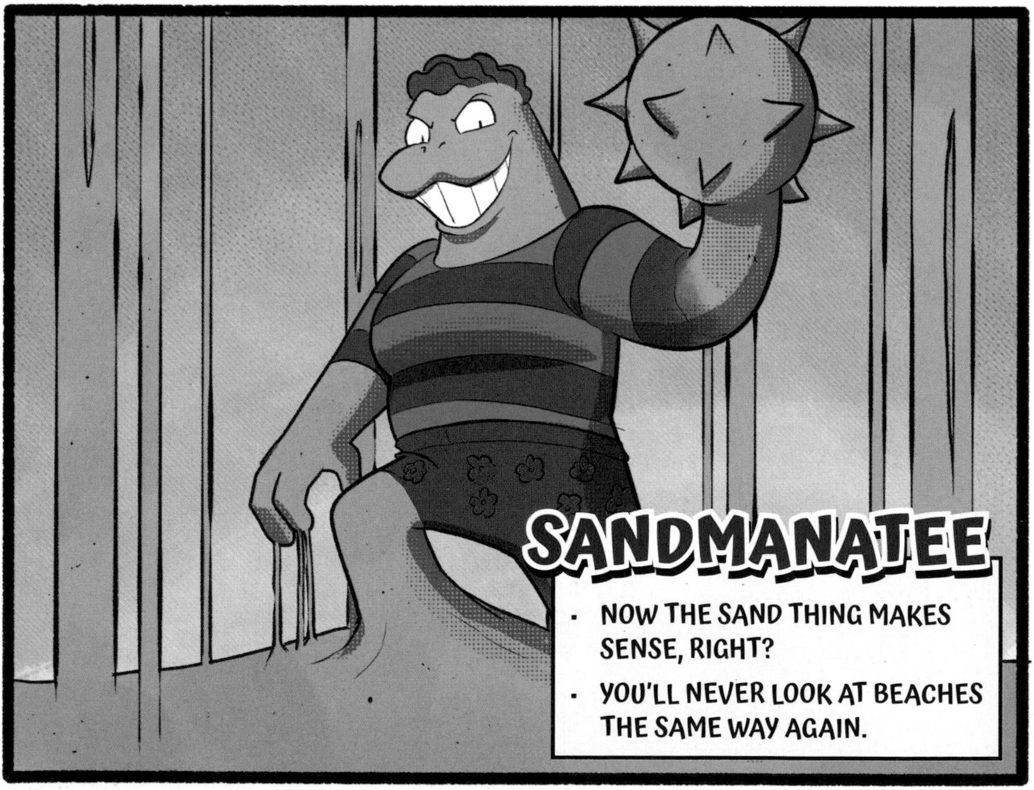
SANDMANATEE
• NOW THE SAND THING MAKES SENSE, RIGHT?
• YOU'LL NEVER LOOK AT BEACHES THE SAME WAY AGAIN.

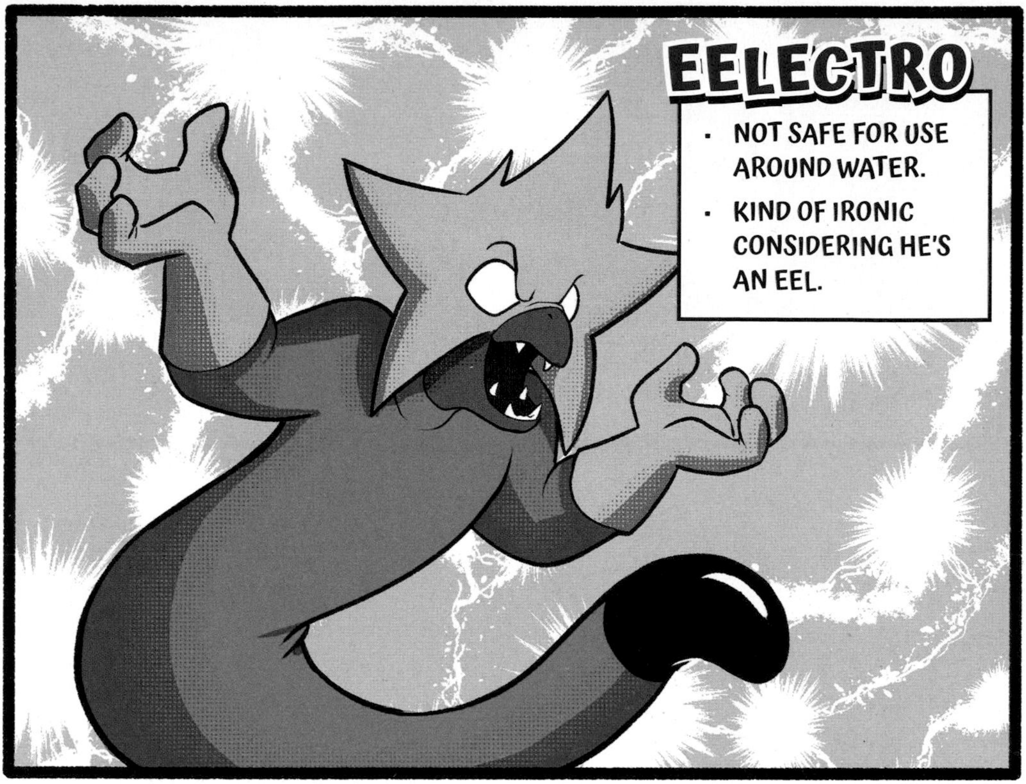
EELECTRO
• NOT SAFE FOR USE AROUND WATER.
• KIND OF IRONIC CONSIDERING HE'S AN EEL.

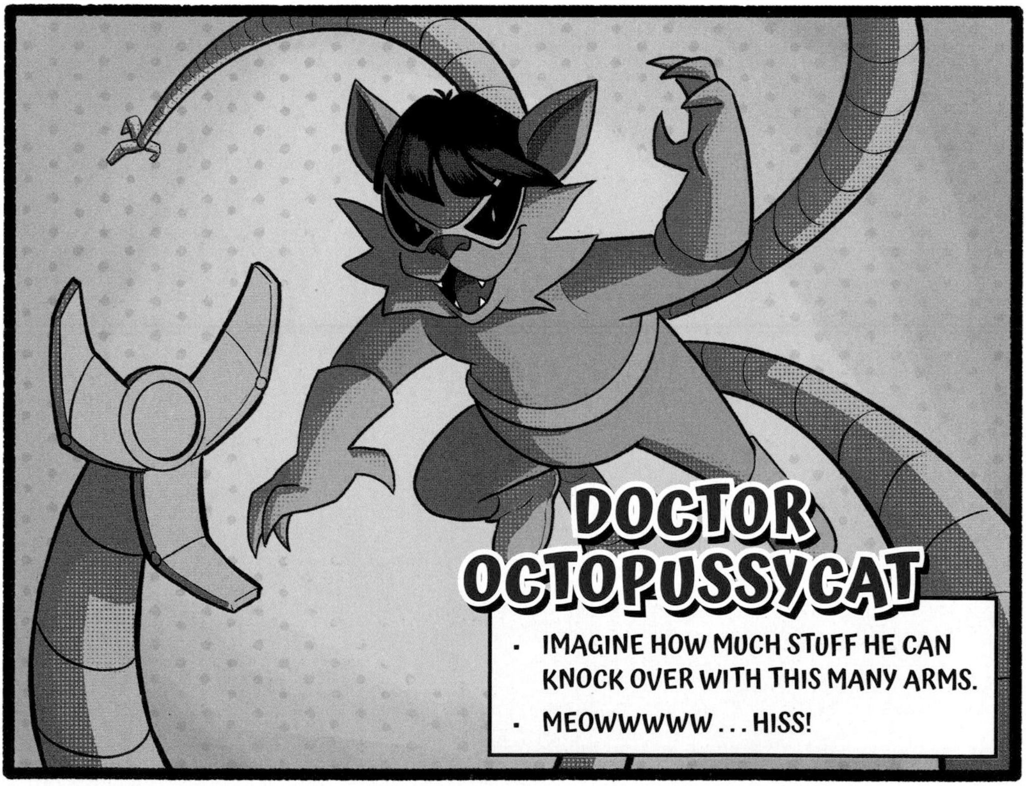
DOCTOR OCTOPUSSYCAT
• IMAGINE HOW MUCH STUFF HE CAN KNOCK OVER WITH THIS MANY ARMS.
• MEOWWWWW . . . HISS!

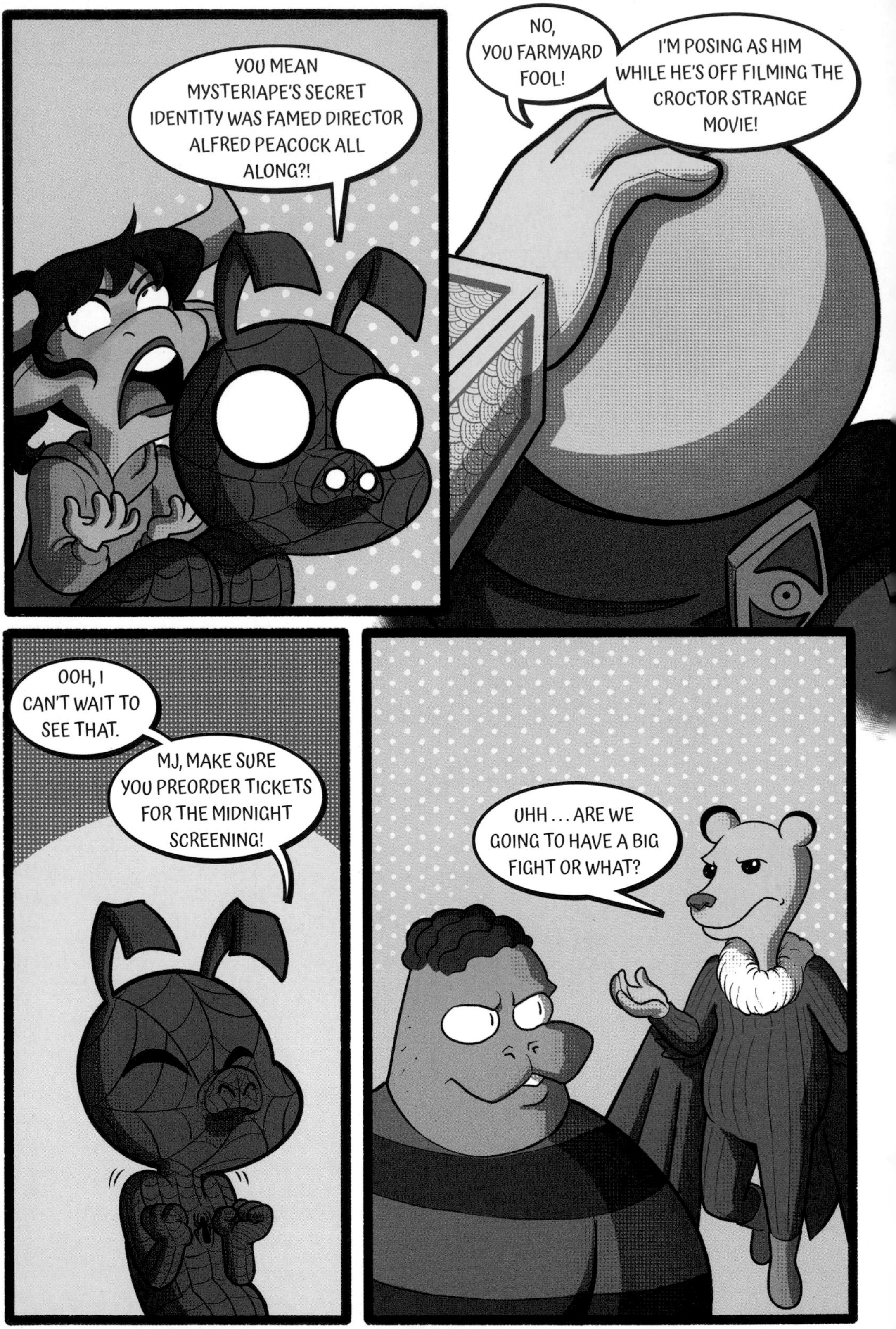
YOU MEAN MYSTERIAPE'S SECRET IDENTITY WAS FAMED DIRECTOR ALFRED PEACOCK ALL ALONG?!
NO, YOU FARMYARD FOOL!
I'M POSING AS HIM WHILE HE'S OFF FILMING THE CROCTOR STRANGE MOVIE!
OOH, I CAN'T WAIT TO SEE THAT.
MJ, MAKE SURE YOU PREORDER TICKETS FOR THE MIDNIGHT SCREENING!
UHH . . . ARE WE GOING TO HAVE A BIG FIGHT OR WHAT?

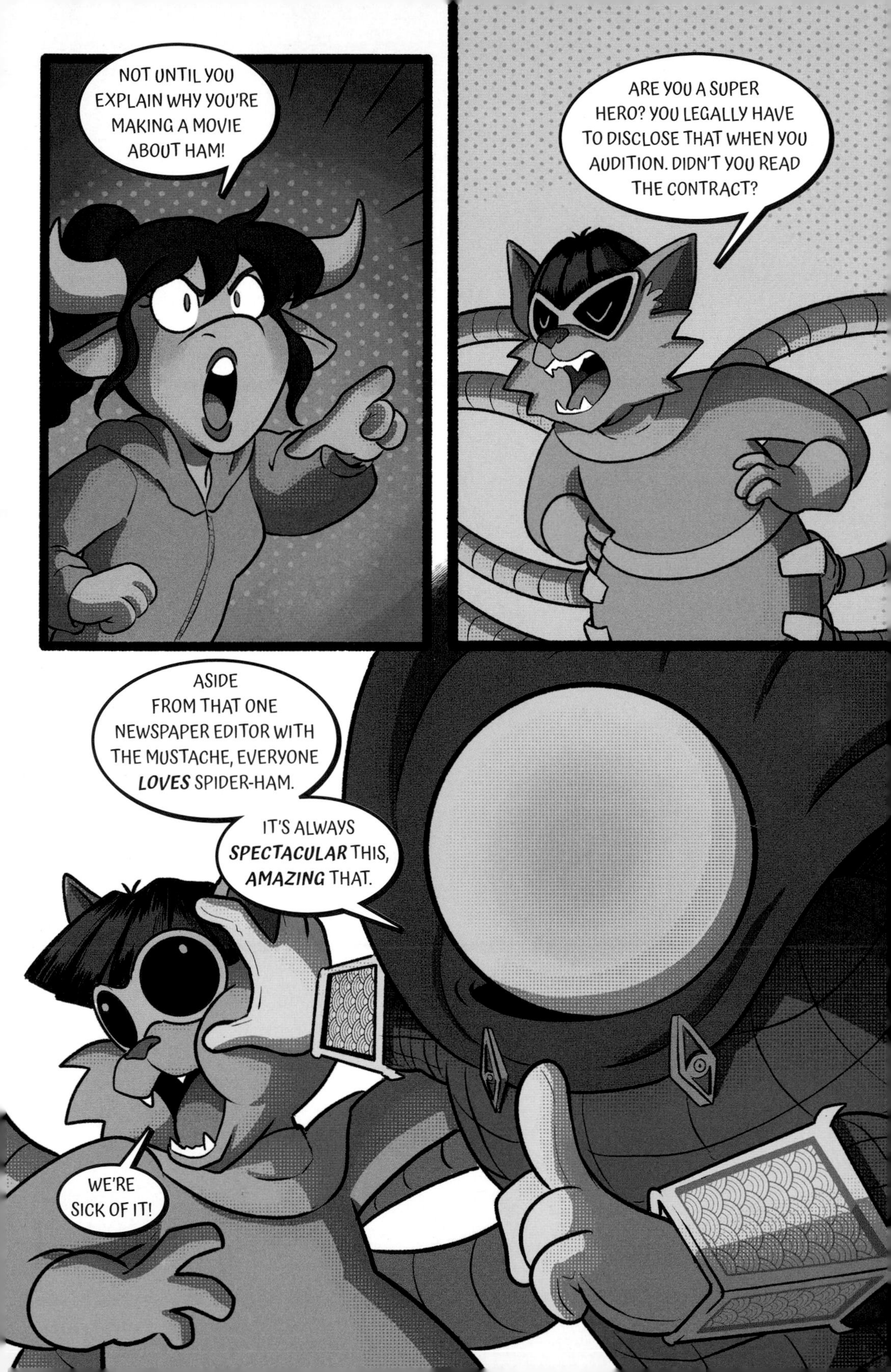
NOT UNTIL YOU EXPLAIN WHY YOU'RE MAKING A MOVIE ABOUT HAM!
ARE YOU A SUPER HERO? YOU LEGALLY HAVE TO DISCLOSE THAT WHEN YOU AUDITION. DIDN'T YOU READ THE CONTRACT?
ASIDE FROM THAT ONE NEWSPAPER EDITOR WITH THE MUSTACHE, EVERYONE **LOVES** SPIDER-HAM.
IT'S ALWAYS **SPECTACULAR** THIS, **AMAZING** THAT.
WE'RE SICK OF IT!

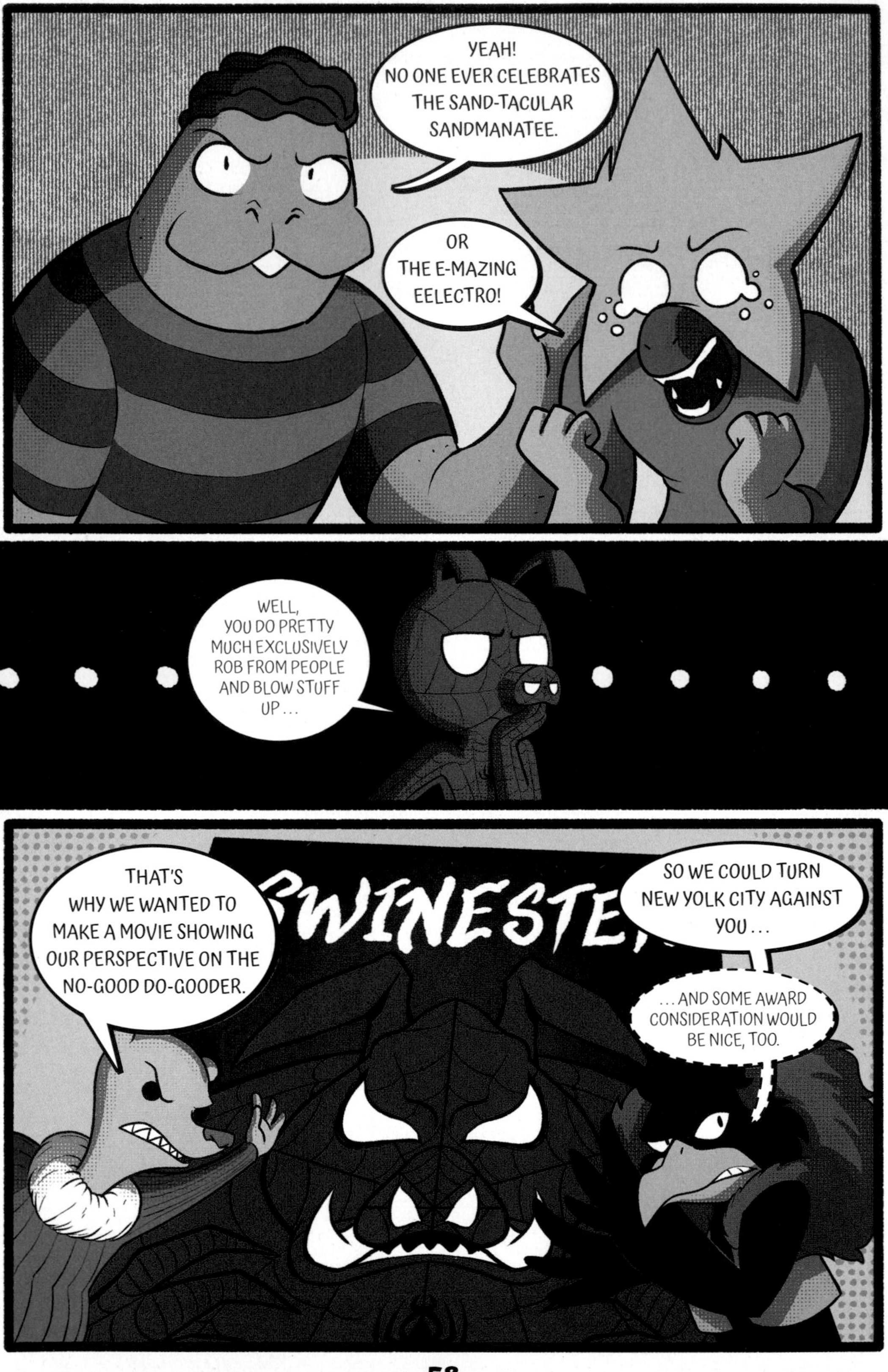
YEAH! NO ONE EVER CELEBRATES THE SAND-TACULAR SANDMANATEE.
OR THE E-MAZING EELECTRO!
WELL, YOU DO PRETTY MUCH EXCLUSIVELY ROB FROM PEOPLE AND BLOW STUFF UP . . .
THAT'S WHY WE WANTED TO MAKE A MOVIE SHOWING OUR PERSPECTIVE ON THE NO-GOOD DO-GOODER.
SWINESTE
SO WE COULD TURN NEW YOLK CITY AGAINST YOU . . .
. . . AND SOME AWARD CONSIDERATION WOULD BE NICE, TOO.

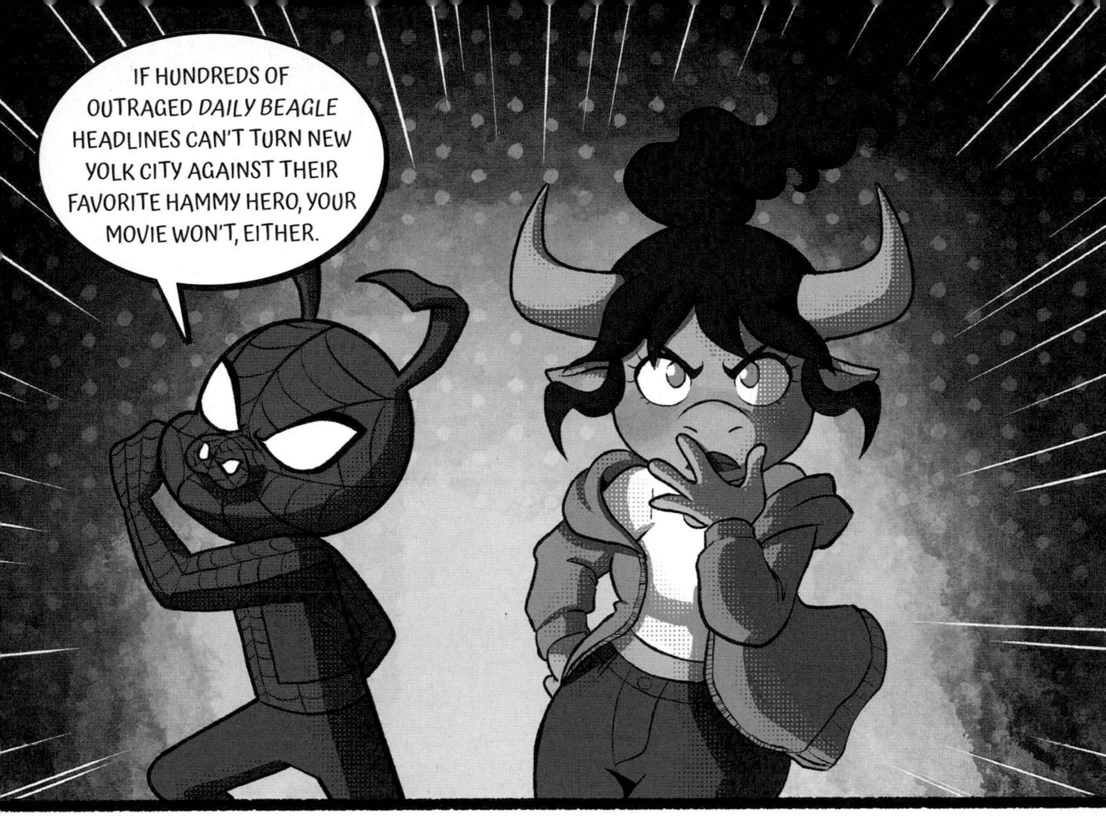
IF HUNDREDS OF OUTRAGED *DAILY BEAGLE* HEADLINES CAN'T TURN NEW YOLK CITY AGAINST THEIR FAVORITE HAMMY HERO, YOUR MOVIE WON'T, EITHER.

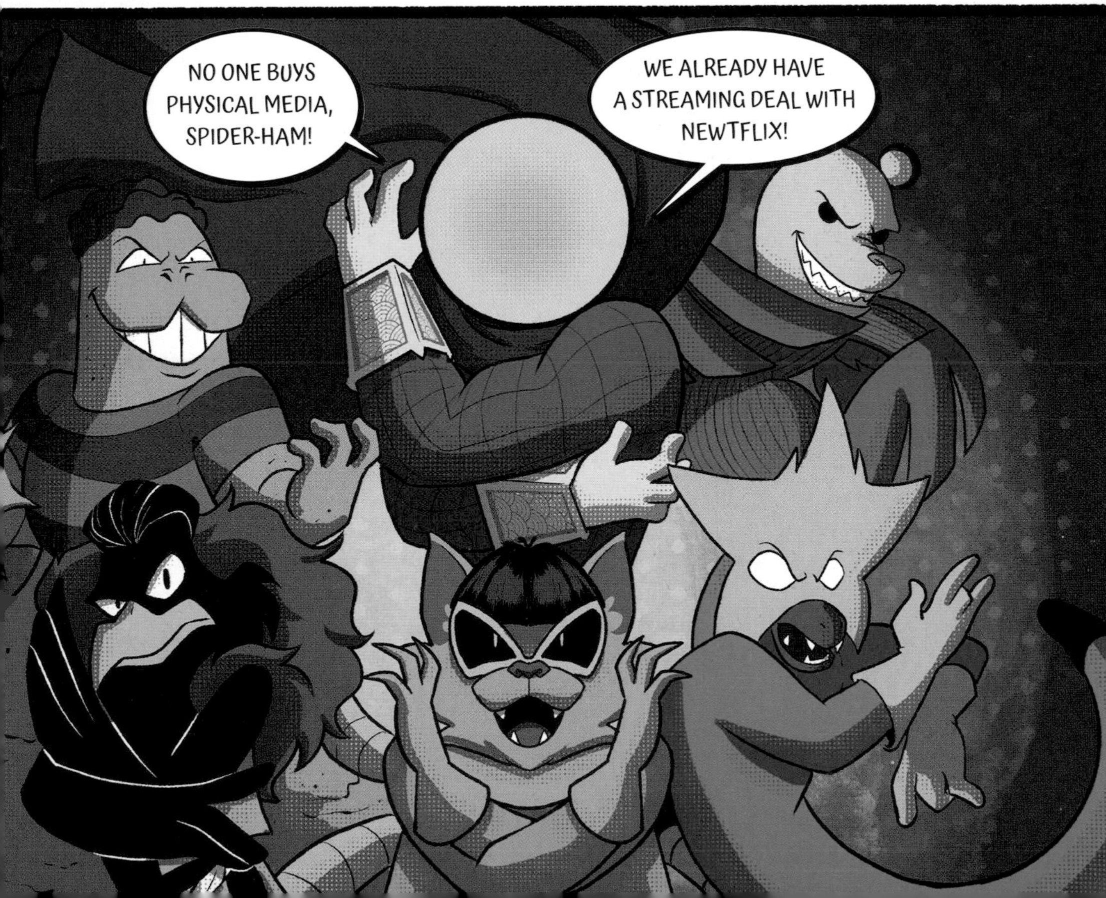
NO ONE BUYS PHYSICAL MEDIA, SPIDER-HAM!
WE ALREADY HAVE A STREAMING DEAL WITH NEWTFLIX!

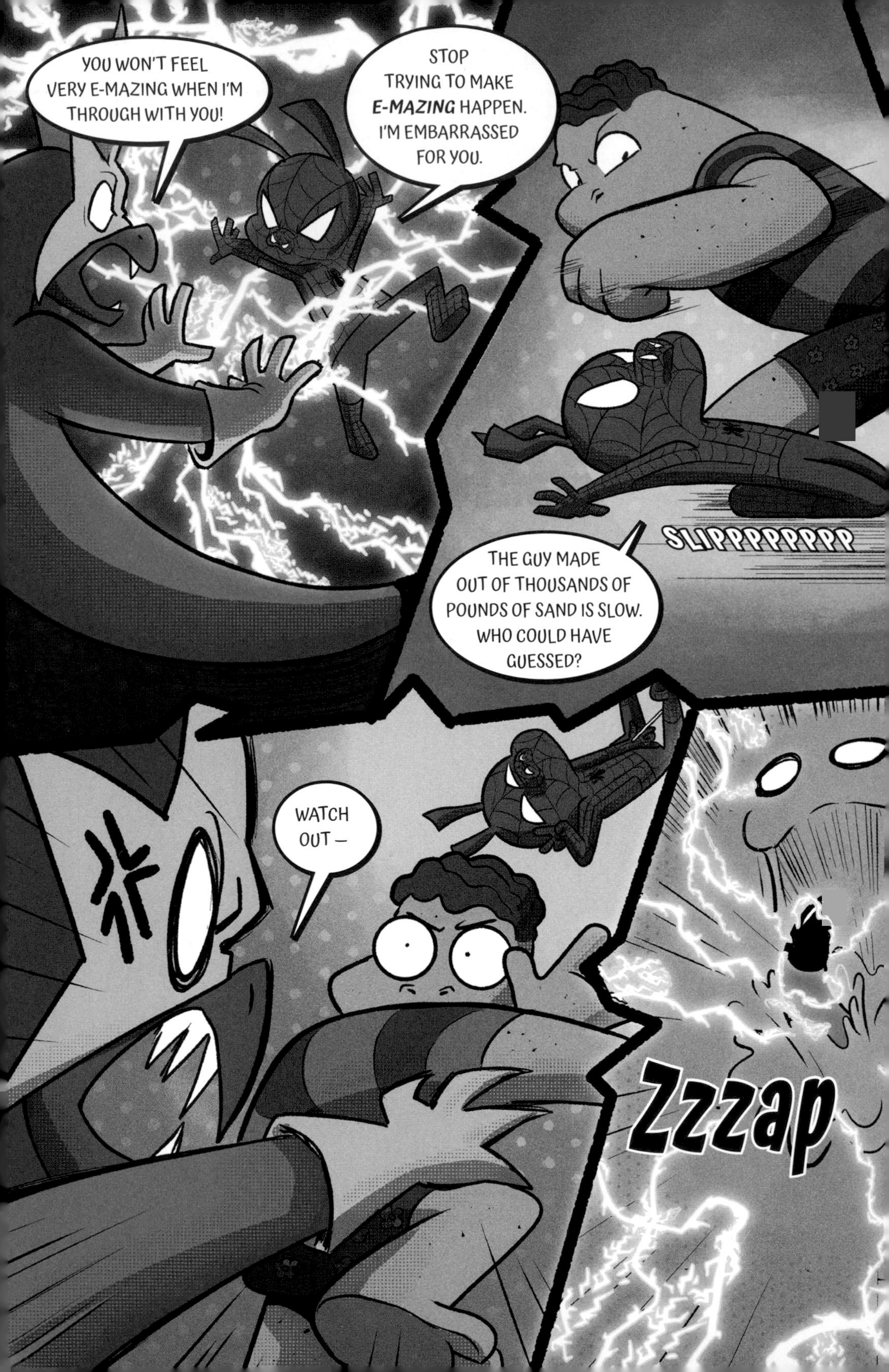
YOU WON'T FEEL VERY E-MAZING WHEN I'M THROUGH WITH YOU!
STOP TRYING TO MAKE **E-MAZING** HAPPEN. I'M EMBARRASSED FOR YOU.
SLIPPPPPPPPP
THE GUY MADE OUT OF THOUSANDS OF POUNDS OF SAND IS SLOW. WHO COULD HAVE GUESSED?
WATCH OUT —
Zzzap

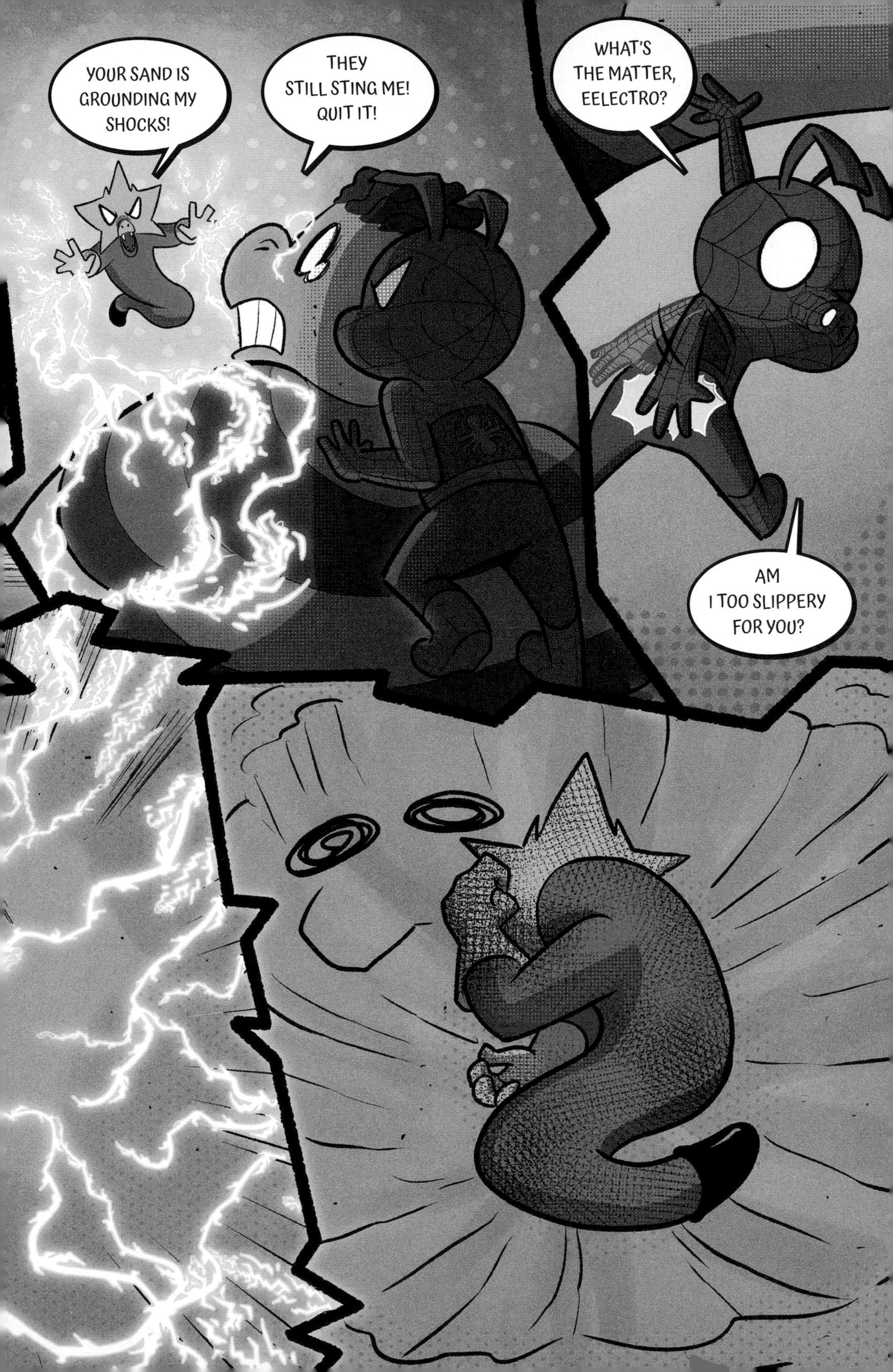
YOUR SAND IS GROUNDING MY SHOCKS!
THEY STILL STING ME! QUIT IT!
WHAT'S THE MATTER, EELECTRO?
AM I TOO SLIPPERY FOR YOU?

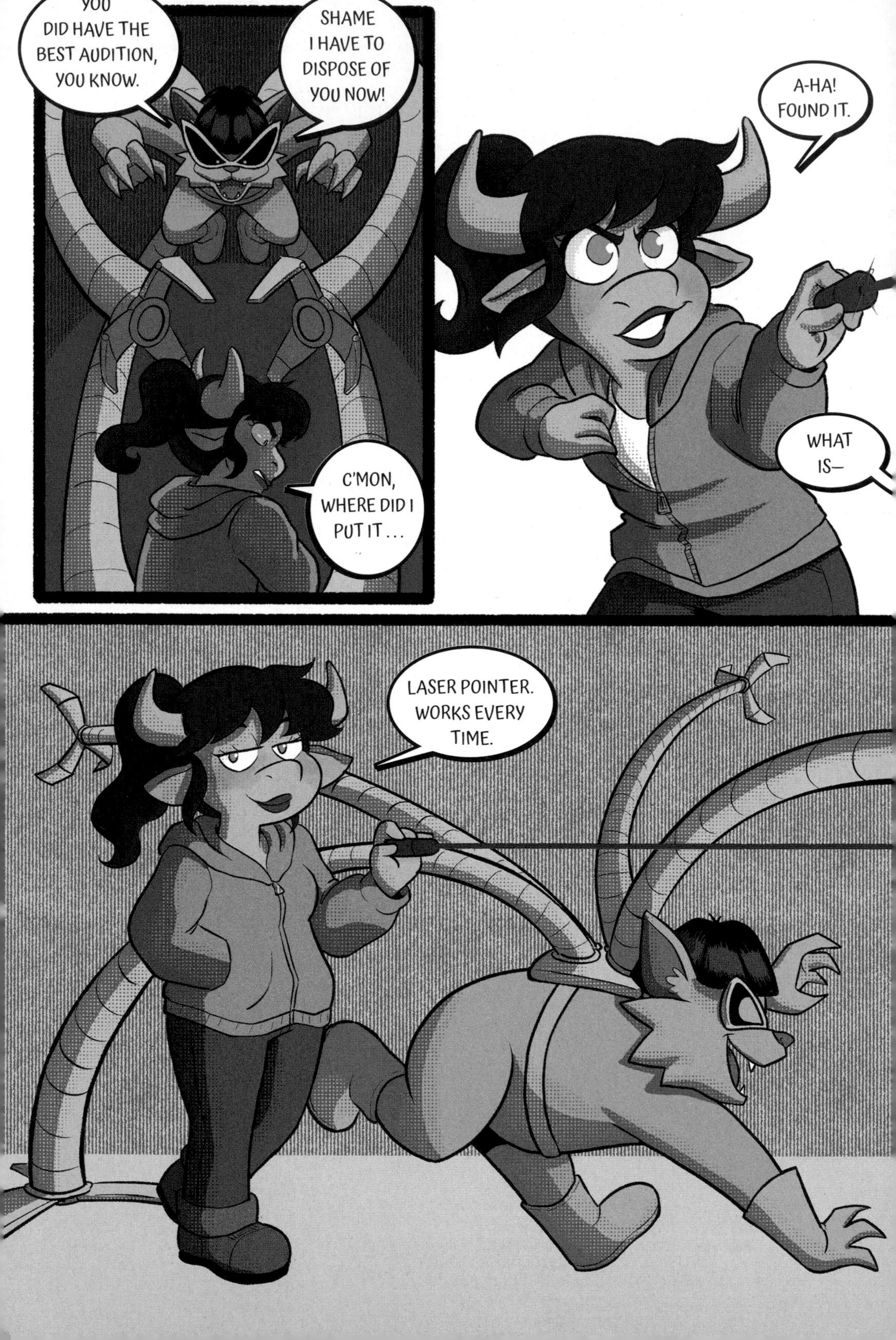
YOU DID HAVE THE BEST AUDITION, YOU KNOW.
SHAME I HAVE TO DISPOSE OF YOU NOW!
C'MON, WHERE DID I PUT IT . . .
A-HA! FOUND IT.
WHAT IS—
LASER POINTER. WORKS EVERY TIME.

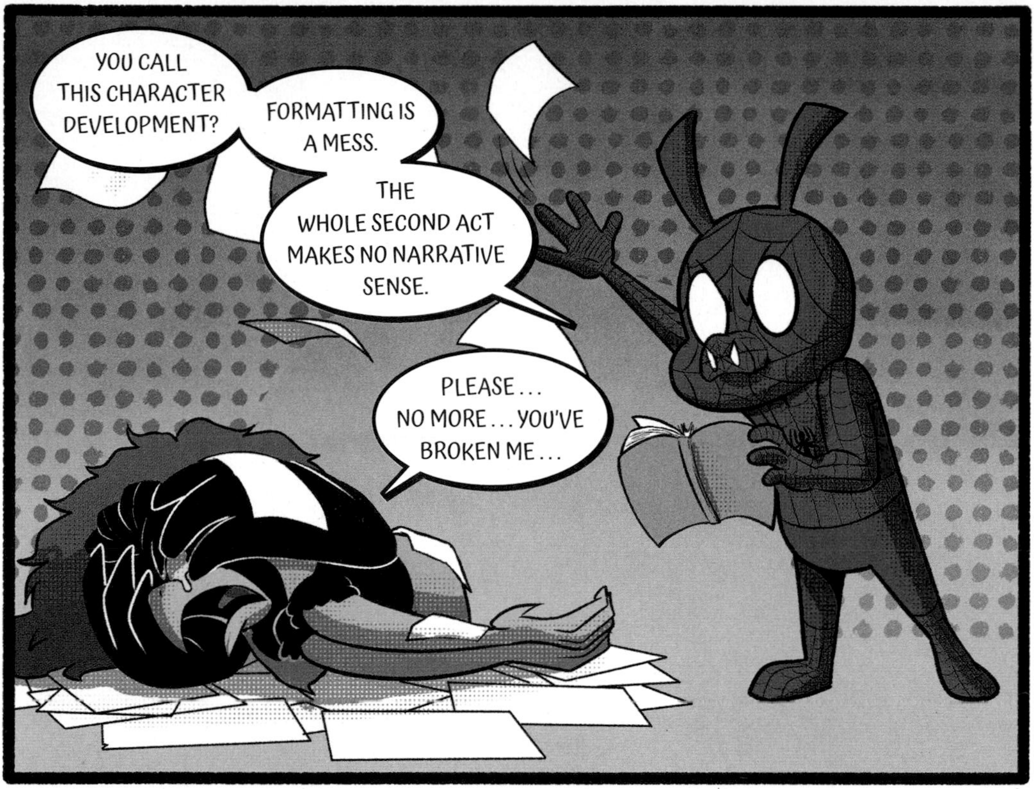
YOU CALL THIS CHARACTER DEVELOPMENT?
FORMATTING IS A MESS.
THE WHOLE SECOND ACT MAKES NO NARRATIVE SENSE.
PLEASE... NO MORE... YOU'VE BROKEN ME...

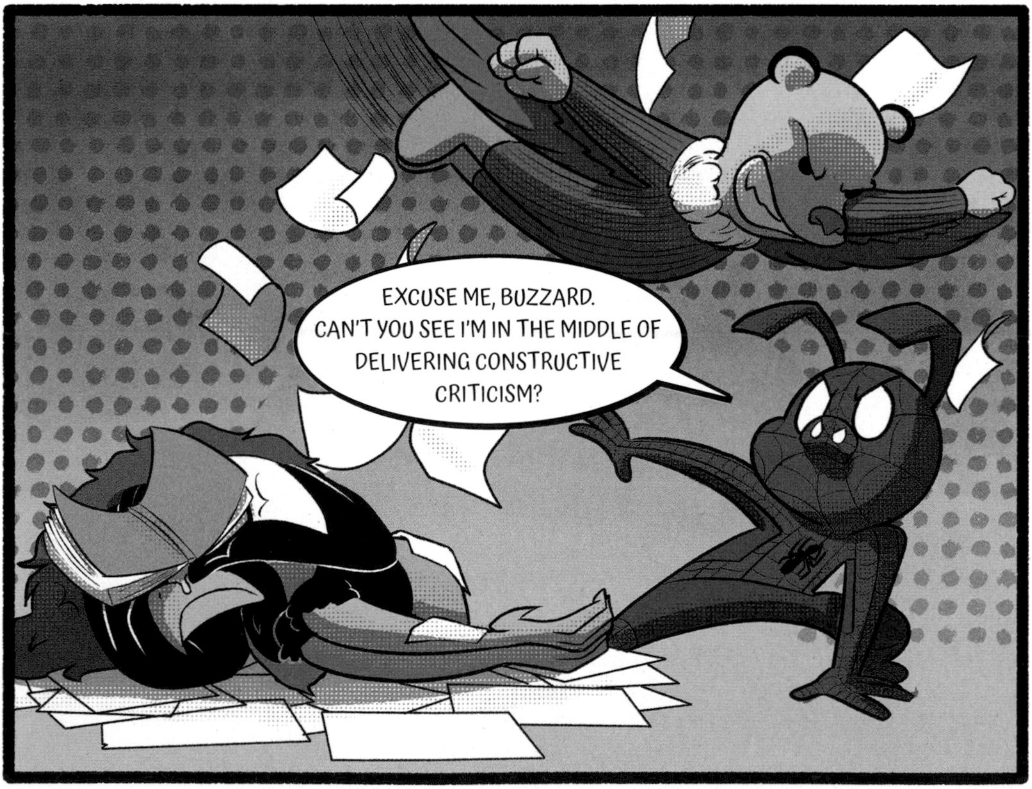
EXCUSE ME, BUZZARD. CAN'T YOU SEE I'M IN THE MIDDLE OF DELIVERING CONSTRUCTIVE CRITICISM?

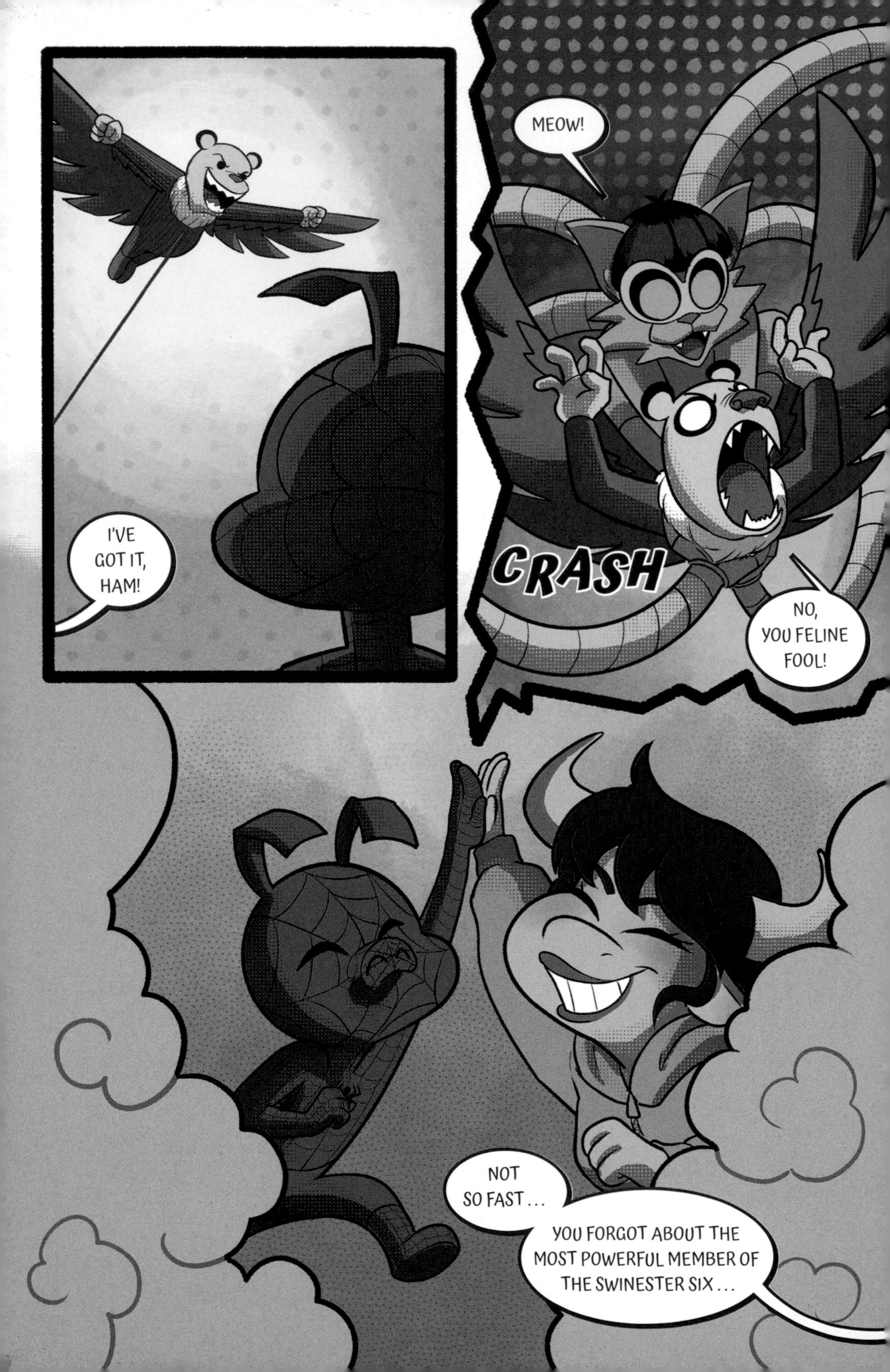

I'VE GOT IT, HAM!
MEOW!
CRASH
NO, YOU FELINE FOOL!
NOT SO FAST . . .
YOU FORGOT ABOUT THE MOST POWERFUL MEMBER OF THE SWINESTER SIX . . .

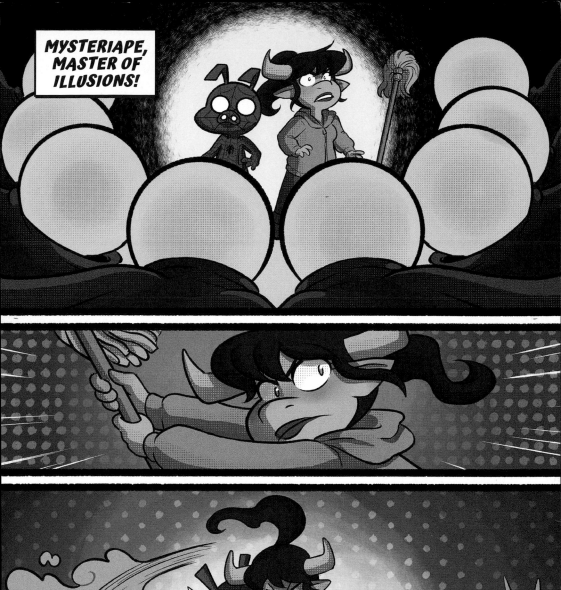

MYSTERIAPE, MASTER OF ILLUSIONS!

HEY, WAIT, DON'T—

CRACK

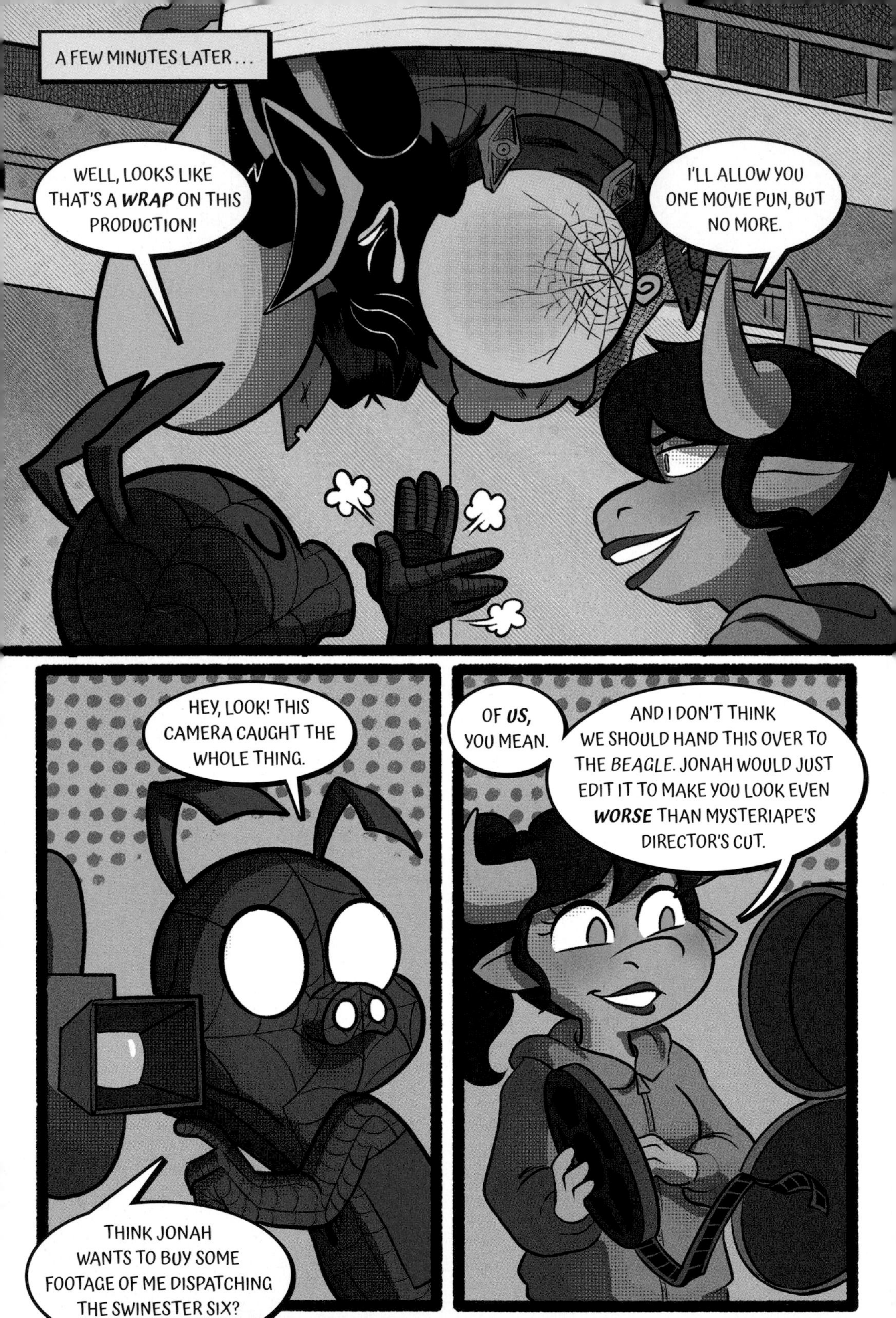
A FEW MINUTES LATER . . .
WELL, LOOKS LIKE THAT'S A ***WRAP*** ON THIS PRODUCTION!
I'LL ALLOW YOU ONE MOVIE PUN, BUT NO MORE.
HEY, LOOK! THIS CAMERA CAUGHT THE WHOLE THING.
THINK JONAH WANTS TO BUY SOME FOOTAGE OF ME DISPATCHING THE SWINESTER SIX?
OF ***US***, YOU MEAN.
AND I DON'T THINK WE SHOULD HAND THIS OVER TO THE *BEAGLE*. JONAH WOULD JUST EDIT IT TO MAKE YOU LOOK EVEN ***WORSE*** THAN MYSTERIAPE'S DIRECTOR'S CUT.

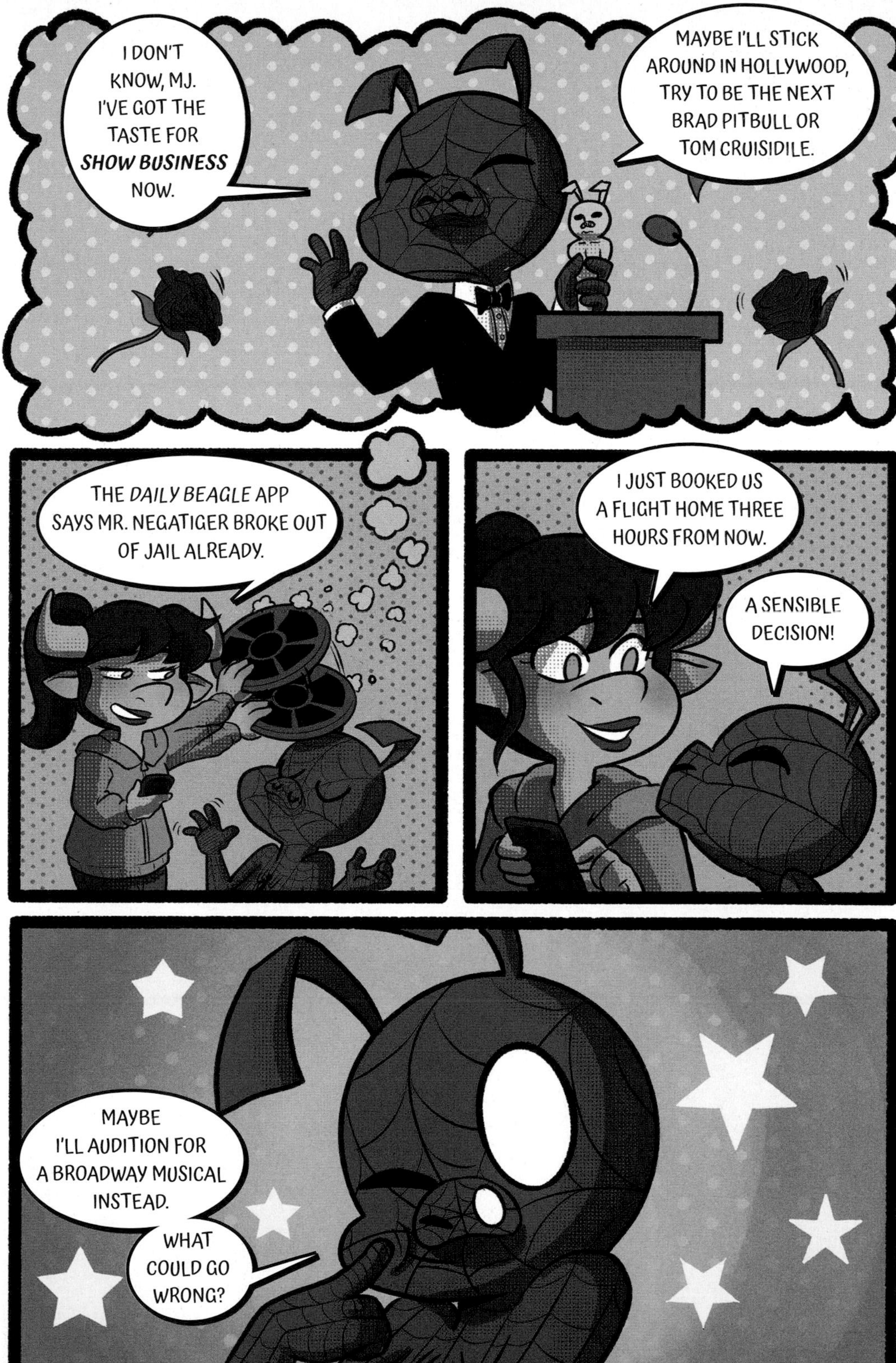
I DON'T KNOW, MJ. I'VE GOT THE TASTE FOR **SHOW BUSINESS** NOW.
MAYBE I'LL STICK AROUND IN HOLLYWOOD, TRY TO BE THE NEXT BRAD PITBULL OR TOM CRUISIDILE.
THE *DAILY BEAGLE* APP SAYS MR. NEGATIGER BROKE OUT OF JAIL ALREADY.
I JUST BOOKED US A FLIGHT HOME THREE HOURS FROM NOW.
A SENSIBLE DECISION!
MAYBE I'LL AUDITION FOR A BROADWAY MUSICAL INSTEAD.
WHAT COULD GO WRONG?

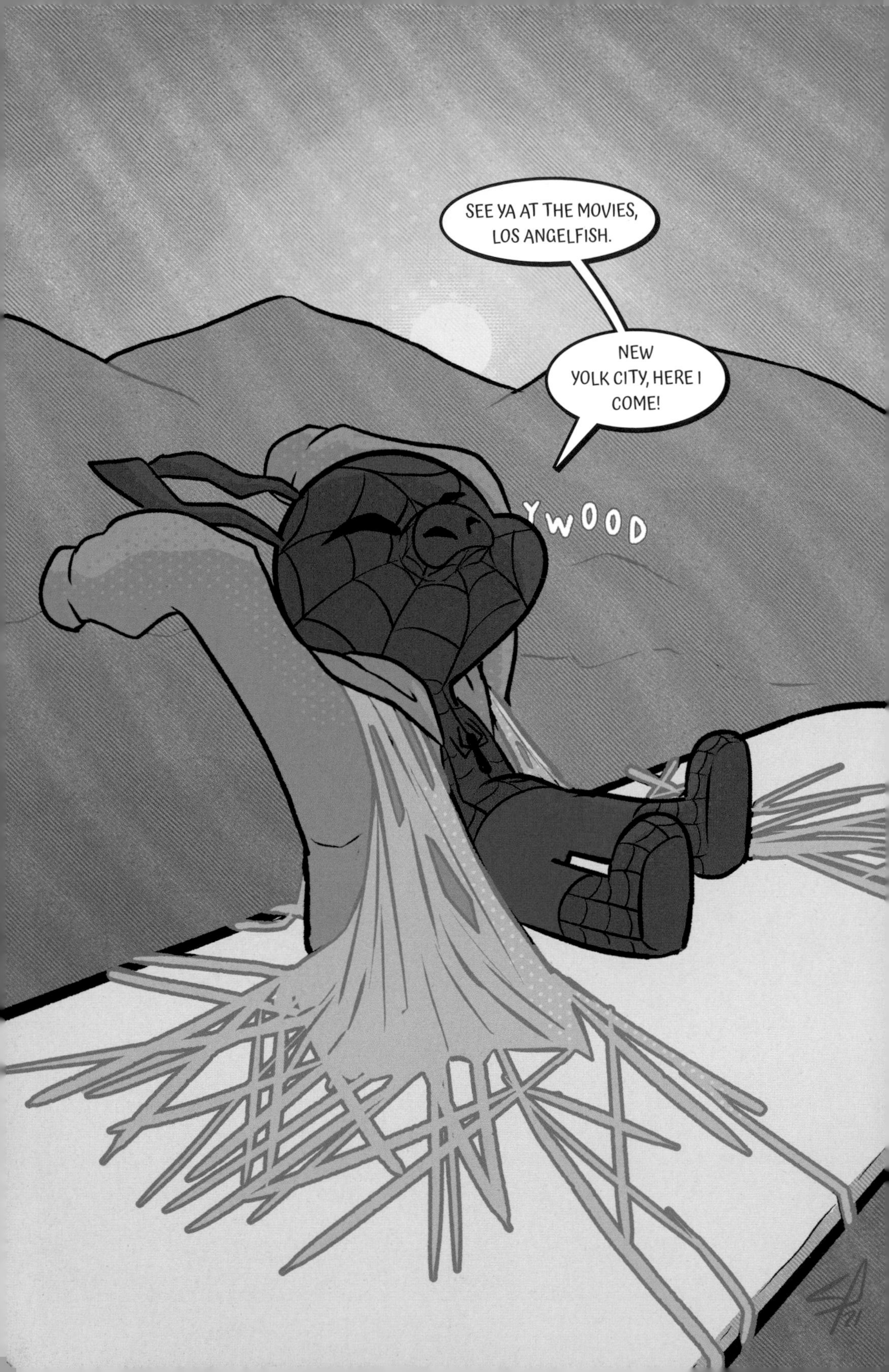
SEE YA AT THE MOVIES, LOS ANGELFISH.
NEW YOLK CITY, HERE I COME!
YWOOD

THE
END

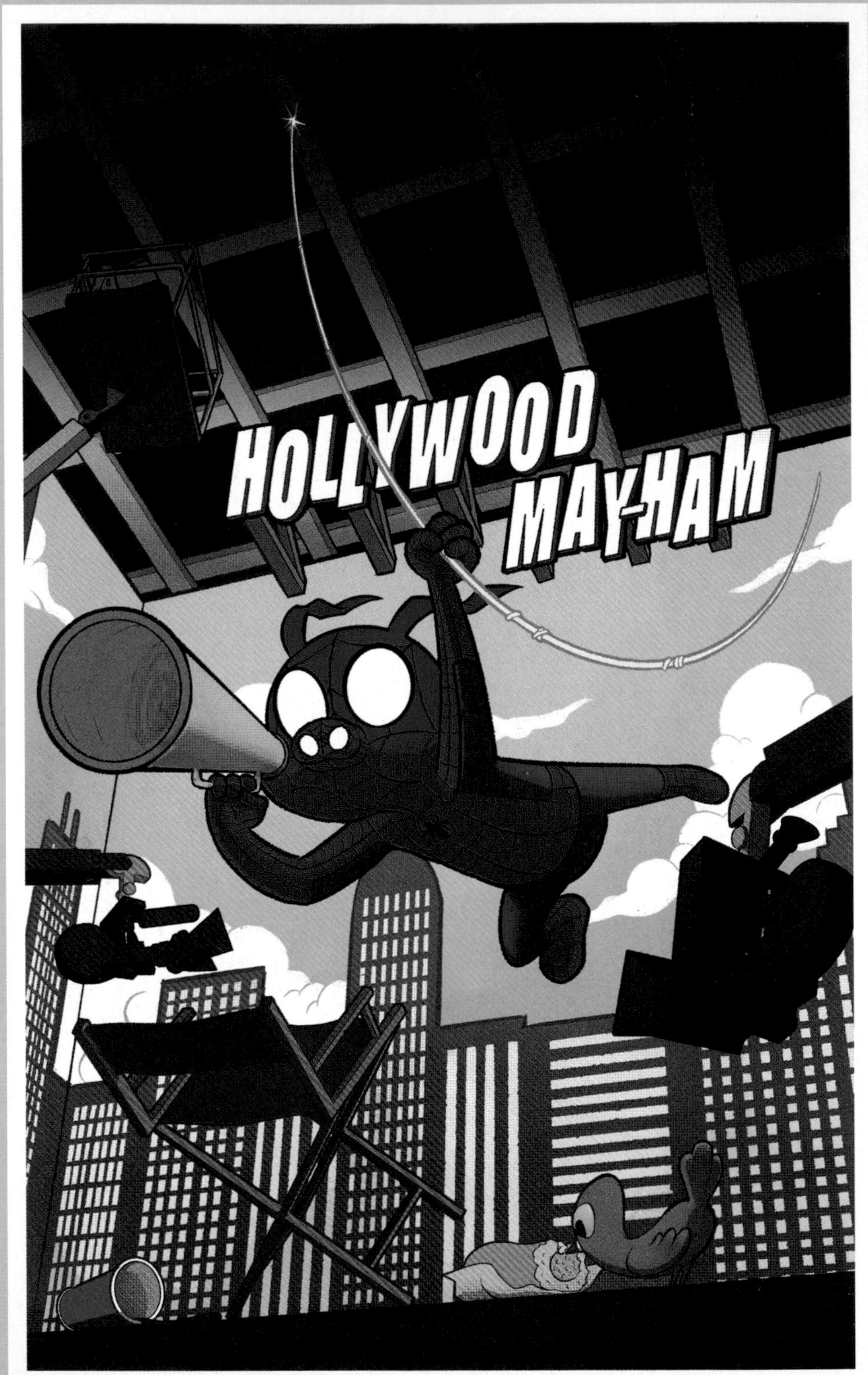
HOLLYWOOD
MAY-HAM

SPOT THE DIFFERENCES: Can you spot the 6 differences?

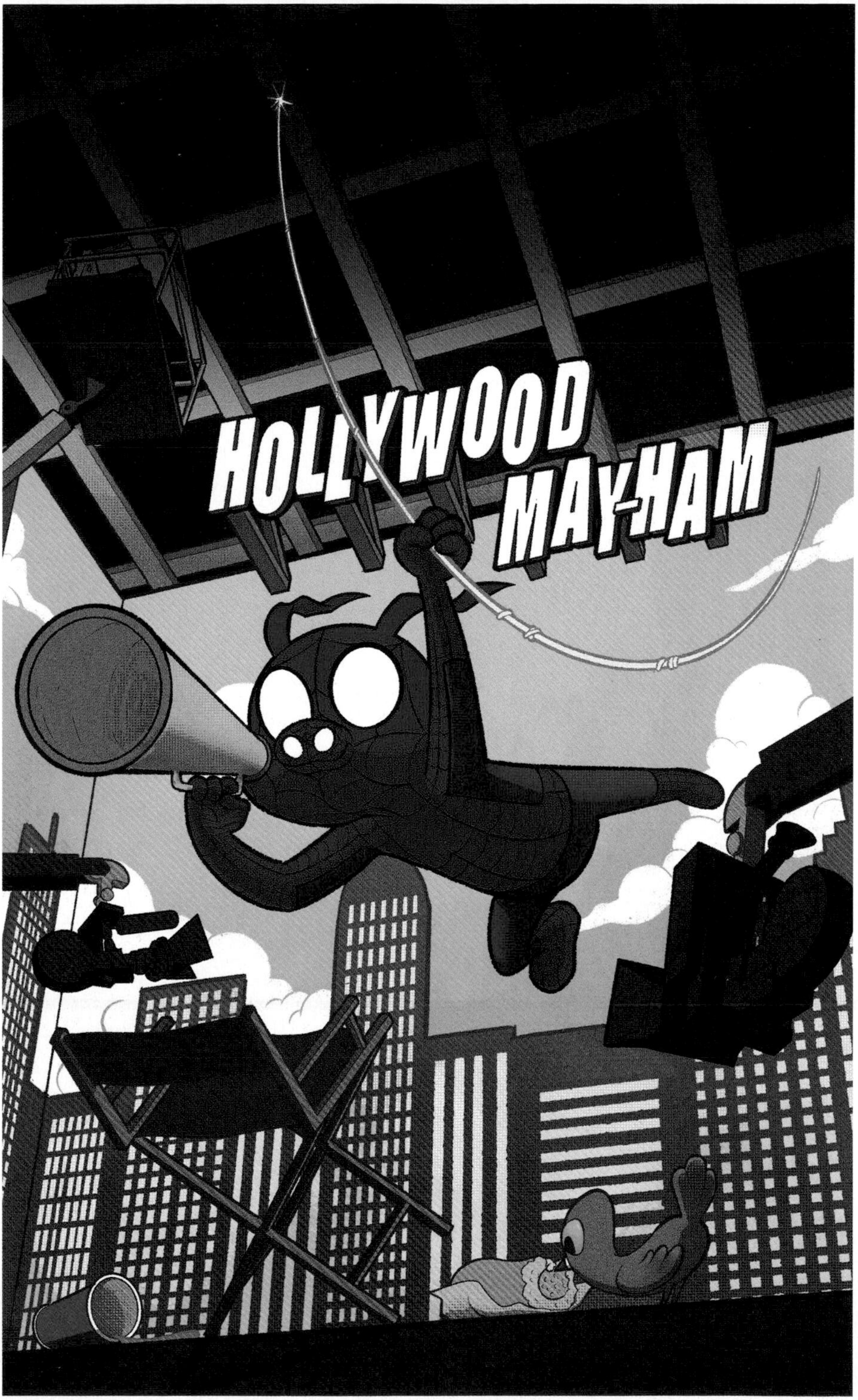
HOLLYWOOD
MAY-HAM

SPECIAL PREVIEW OF

Avengers Assembly #3: X-Change Students 101

CHAPTER 1

FROM: Miles Morales <mmorales0811@heatmail.com>

TO: Kamala Khan <k-khan2014@heatmail.com>;
Doreen Green <acornluvr@heatmail.com>;
Evan Sabahnur <evan_sabahnur@heatmail.com>

FWD: Extended Field Trip to Xavier's School for Gifted Youngsters

WE'RE TAKIN' A TRIP! Also how does Principal Danvers ignore every single x-quisite pun opportunity in this email. It hurts my brain.

Miles

FROM: Carol Danvers <cdanvers@avengers-institute.com>

TO: Avengers Institute Exchange Students <exchange-avengers-student-list-serv@avengers-institute.com>

Subject: Extended Field Trip to Xavier's School for Gifted Youngsters

Hello students,

We're very pleased to announce a field trip opportunity for students. A small group of second-years will be heading to Xavier's School for Gifted Youngsters to learn from the X-Men. We've contacted your families with a cover story as well as legitimate contact information should anything unexpected happen.

Please remember that you are representing Avengers Institute and act accordingly. You'll find a packing guide and itinerary attached to this email.

Groups will arrive at staggered times, so please check your itinerary carefully.

Col. Carol Danvers
Principal, Avengers Institute

MILES'S JOURNAL

IT IS SLEEPAWAY CAMP TIME.
Kind of! We're back for a new
semester at Avengers Institute, but
all anyone is talking about is our two-
week camp at the X-Mansion.

(You could say we're <u>X-cited</u>. No, I
won't be limiting my X-puns for this
X-cellent adventure.)

Ganke knows where I'll be—but my
parents think I'm going to a highly
prestigious, rigorous academic program
for exceptional students.

I guess you could change that to
"<u>X-ceptional</u>" and it would be mostly
true, huh?

I wonder how K's getting out of her
house for two weeks—Doreen's parents
know about her, uh, night job (Which

is wild!! My mom would never let me leave my room again if she knew the kind of stuff we got into—I was in a pocket dimension last semester!), and Evan's actually from Xavier's. Hmmm. We should ask Evan about the coolest hang spots. And if there's even decent pizza in Connecticut (that's where Westchester is, right?).

I wonder who else is coming on this trip—and what we're going to learn?? Beast's class was pretty cool, but I want to see what the other X-Men have to offer. Oh man, if Wolverine is teaching us, I am going to sit in the very front of the class.

This is going to be so cool!!!!!

Now I just have to pack—we're leaving in a few hours, and my bags are e m p t y.

XAVIER'S SCHEMOOL FOR GIFTED YOUNGSTERS

❏ **One Avengers Institute X-Change uniform**

I knew the X-Men wouldn't let us down!!

❏ **Shower shoes & caddy**

Are the showers . . . communal??
Can I shower with my mask on?
Note to self: Talk to the other Spidey

❏ **Your Avengers Institute communicators**

❏ **Train tickets**

. . . We're not just going to teleport there?
We have to take the Metro-North???

❏ **Laundry detergent**

We have to do <u>laundry</u>?!
Do I need to bring . . . quarters?

MILES'S NOTES

Avengers Institute Exchange Program Itinerary

Trip to Westchester:

10:30 AM: Meet at Grand Central Station at the Big Clock

11:11 AM: Depart for Westchester, NY, on the Metro-North Rail

12:33 PM: Arrive in Westchester, NY—Professor Kate Pryde will be waiting for the students to bring them to Xavier's School

1:00 PM: X-change student orientation

1:30 PM: Schedules and dorm assignments distributed

2:00 PM—Evening: Free time

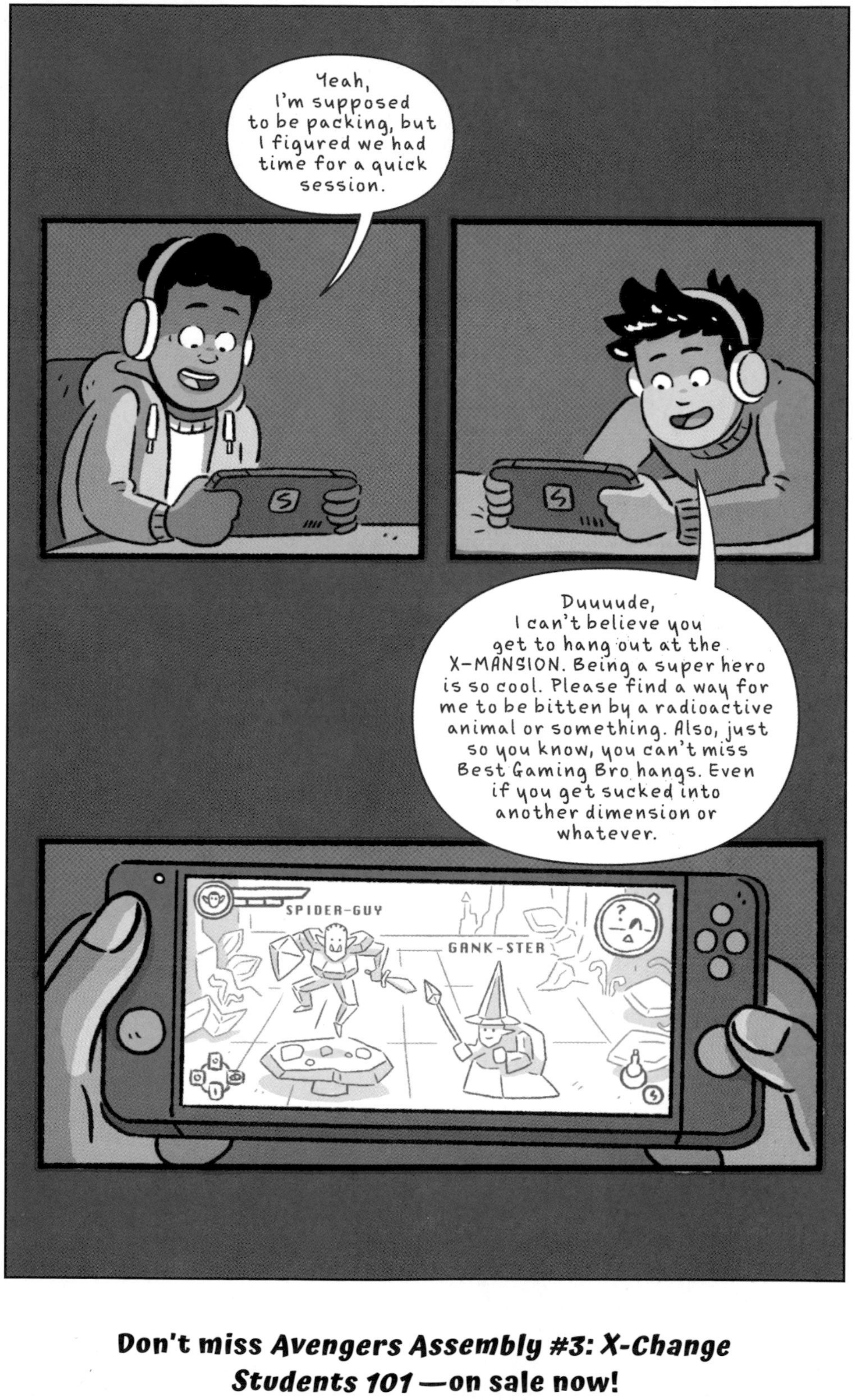
Yeah, I'm supposed to be packing, but I figured we had time for a quick session.
Duuuude, I can't believe you get to hang out at the X-MANSION. Being a super hero is so cool. Please find a way for me to be bitten by a radioactive animal or something. Also, just so you know, you can't miss Best Gaming Bro hangs. Even if you get sucked into another dimension or whatever.
SPIDER-GUY
GANK-STER

Don't miss *Avengers Assembly #3: X-Change Students 101* —on sale now!

STEVE FOXE is the author of more than fifty comics and children's books for properties including Pokémon, Batman, Transformers, Adventure Time, Steven Universe, and Grumpy Cat. He lives in Queens with his partner and their dog, who is named after a cartoon character. He does not eat ham. Find out more at stevefoxe.com.

SHADIA AMIN is a Colombian comics artist currently living in the United States. Her art aims to capture the fun of super heroes, fantasy, and life itself. Her works include BOOM!'s *The Amazing World of Gumball: The Storm*, Oni–Lion Forge's *Aggretsuko*, as well as collaborations on anthologies like *Electrum*, produced by the Alloy Anthology and published by Ascend Comics, and *Votes for Women*, published by Little Red Bird Press. Burgers are to her what hot dogs are to Spider-Ham.